Affronted, Lydia straightened. "I am not lonely. I've been to many parties . . . when I was in London. You would be amazed at how sociable I can be. Sometimes there were three in one night."

"You are not in London now." His face was very close to hers. She could see the plane of his cheek, the strength of his chin, and the lashes outlining his eyes. Tenderness filled them—and something more.

She paused before whispering, "No, I am not."

And then her breath caught.

Their faces were scant inches apart. The woods became exceedingly still. The birds hushed their songs. Even the buzz of the insects quieted. It was as if nature joined Lydia in holding her breath—waiting.

He bent forward. With the lightest of touches, his lips brushed over hers. His stroke was gentle and sweet, a true example of his nature. When he lifted his head, a fleeting regret flashed through her. Her taste of him had been too short. She curved her lips into an invitation. . . .

The Winter Duke

Louise Bergin

A SIGNET BOOK

SIGNET
Published by New American Library, a division of
Penguin Group (USA) Inc., 375 Hudson Street,
New York, New York 10014, USA
Penguin Group (Canada), 10 Alcorn Avenue, Toronto,
Ontario M4V 3B2, Canada (a division of Pearson Penguin Canada Inc.)
Penguin Books Ltd., 80 Strand, London WC2R 0RL, England
Penguin Ireland, 25 St. Stephen's Green, Dublin 2,
Ireland (a division of Penguin Books, Ltd.)
Penguin Group (Australia), 250 Camberwell Road, Camberwell, Victoria 3124,
Australia (a division of Pearson Australia Group Pty. Ltd.)
Penguin Books India Pvt. Ltd., 11 Community Centre, Panchsheel Park,
New Delhi - 110 017, India
Penguin Group (NZ), cnr Airborne and Rosedale Roads, Albany,
Auckland 1310, New Zealand (a division of Pearson New Zealand Ltd.)
Penguin Books (South Africa) (Pty.) Ltd., 24 Sturdee Avenue,
Rosebank, Johannesburg 2196, South Africa

Penguin Books Ltd., Registered Offices:
80 Strand, London WC2R 0RL, England

First published by Signet, an imprint of New American Library,
a division of Penguin Group (USA) Inc.

First Printing, April 2005
10 9 8 7 6 5 4 3 2 1

For my mother-in-law,
Esther Bergin.
Thank you for the gift of your son Joe.

Chapter One

*M*iss Lydia Grenville returned home from her London Season a failure at nineteen years of age. No one at Grenville Manor or throughout the surrounding countryside of Essex was bold enough to call her one to her face, but she recognized what people's thoughts were in the way their glances slid away from hers and in how no one asked about her Season.

Lydia had plenty of memorable parties to recall, fabulous balls to discuss, and well-attended dinners to talk about. Yet no one approached the topic of her Season. She couldn't blame them. People shied away from failure, fearing it would taint or curse them somehow. She wanted to rail against her fate, but such a tantrum would do her no good. Besides, she knew she had not accomplished the task life had prepared her for. She was not betrothed.

She was well versed in the arts of drawing, dancing, and pianoforte. With her golden ringlets, smooth complexion, and distinguished, if not spectacular, dowry, Lydia should have at least returned as the betrothed of an earl. She had received offers, but those suitors had either been well-known fortune hunters or not appropriate in either rank or fortune. Or—and Lydia would admit this only to herself—the man's personal habits had been nothing to recommend him. She wanted something more from her marriage. She knew better than to expect love. Instead, she hoped for companionship such as her father and mother possessed.

Her parents had allowed her to reject adequate suitors, but they could not completely hide their disappointment. She had hurt them by her failure.

The worst encounters occurred during the calls upon the neighbors. It seemed to Lydia that along with the tea and biscuits, her deficits were served on the platters.

The afternoon at the Chandler house, the matrons chattered while Lydia was subjected to the courtesies of Miss Elizabeth, the daughter of the house. The other girl possessed luxuriant brown hair and striking features but lacked Lydia's advantages of dowry and town bronze. Elizabeth also expected to succeed when her Season arrived. Lydia braced herself for the polite needling.

Elizabeth sipped her tea. "My parents have told me that my aunt will be guiding me through my London Season next spring. Perhaps you met her, Lydia?"

"Yes, I met Lady Chandler at several functions and attended the musicale she held at her home." Lydia stiffened her spine. This young lady paused in a conversation only when laying a trap for the unwary.

"A musicale, yes." The other girl tittered. "When I make my come-out, she will host a ball in my honor. She will invite only the most eligible of men because she is my aunt."

"How very good of her," Lydia murmured.

"Since you are my friend, I will see that you receive an invitation." Elizabeth paused again for effect. "Will you be having a second Season?"

"Why would I not?"

"The expense can be so great, and to not take . . ." Shaking her head, Elizabeth offered her pity.

Stung, Lydia retorted, "I had offers."

"I know, but when they are not acceptable . . ." She shook her head again.

Only her unyielding training in deportment prevented Lydia from flinging her tea at the other girl. She bit her tongue instead. A proper lady did not boast of her proposals.

It was not only Elizabeth. It was also the girl's mother, and indeed all the county's matrons, who eyed her askance. Lydia held her head high against the tiny barbs flung her way. Although she would never admit they struck their target, the pain still existed.

Even her own bedroom provided no sanctuary. Lydia sat before her looking glass, remembering a Venetian breakfast where she'd laughed with a dandified sprig of nobility. What was his name?

Her maid interrupted her daydreaming. "Miss, what dress would you like to wear today?"

Meg was a woman several years older than Lydia, with heavy brows and brown hair she wore captured in a tight bun at the nape of her neck. Despite her severe appearance, she knew her trade. Her mistress never left her boudoir without being a credit to Meg's skill.

Lydia brushed her hair to smooth the kinks left by the night's braids. "The blue-sprigged one, please."

"That is a very pretty dress for the country."

With her hairbrush raised, Lydia glanced at Meg. Had there been emphasis on the word *country*? "Its style is all the rage in the city. The mantua-maker in London made it for me. I happen to know Lady Sophia Godfrey had copied the pattern, and she never leaves London."

"Yes, miss. The seamstress did her job well."

Meg took the dress from the wardrobe and laid it on the bed. The neckline was appropriate for daywear. A blue satin ribbon tied under the high bodice, and tiny puffed sleeves displayed Lydia's arms to an advantage. It was one of her favorite dresses. Some of her suitors had claimed its blue flowers matched the color of her eyes. She privately agreed with them.

Meg helped Lydia put on the dress and then curled her mistress's hair. When she was finished, Lydia inspected the result in her looking glass.

Satisfied, she said, "That will do very well. Thank you, Meg."

The maid swept the remaining hairpins into a small pile. "You look just like a portrait of a country miss. A very pretty one."

Lydia's smile became more fixed. Had Meg's comment held a hidden meaning? Or was Lydia now reduced to finding insults in compliments? Had her failed Season made her too sensitive to commonplace remarks?

With her chin lifted, she swept from her bedroom and went down to breakfast. She did not need these reminders that she lived in the country. Yes, Grenville Manor in Essex was her home and had been since her birth. Raised behind its sheltering walls, she was the cosseted only child of Josiah and Katherine Grenville. They showered her with pretty gowns, gentle horses, and lessons in drawing, singing, and deportment—all the skills a girl needed to ensnare an eligible *parti*. A good marriage had been expected, a brilliant one predicted.

She had left Grenville Manor with great fanfare for London and her Season. She had tiptoed home.

With a subdued demeanor, Lydia slipped into the dining room. Her father was already engrossed in the newspaper as he tackled his eggs and herring. Her mother smiled a greeting when Lydia kissed her on the cheek. With blond curls and blue eyes, the mother looked like an older image of her daughter. She had taken great care of herself throughout the years, and the results showed. Lydia intended to emulate her example.

She sat, and the footman brought her a plate with the single muffin she usually ate. One must be careful not to overeat and ruin one's figure. A pleasing appearance was a lady's most noticeable resource.

"What do you plan for today?" her mother asked.

"I had not really thought. Perhaps I will go sketching."

Her mother stirred her tea with her spoon. "You could visit Fanny. I am certain your friend would appreciate a call."

"She probably would." Whatever else she did today, Lydia would not include visiting Fanny in her plans. The girl would want to hear all about London—and she would ask point-blank about Lydia's lack of success.

"Fanny should be out of mourning by now."

Lydia nibbled a piece of her muffin. "Yes, it has been over a year since the duke's death."

"Such a tragedy," her mother murmured.

"A tragedy? It's an outrage!" Her father pounded the table.

Startled, Lydia looked at her father.

He shook his newspaper. "These press gangs. Taking good yeomen and forcing them to serve in the Navy. It's an outrage. It should be stopped."

"Oh, Papa, not now."

From over his newspaper, he glowered at her. "It's our duty to care about those under us."

She did not want to hear more speeches about her duty.

"Must we discuss this at breakfast? Surely the library is the more appropriate place?"

His round face softened. "I suppose you're right, poppet. You're much too young and pretty for this. Such ugliness should never cross your path. Sorry I got carried away."

Lydia smiled her forgiveness. She could always charm her father out of his grumps.

Much more jovially, her father said, "Did I hear you tell your mother you were going to call on Fanny today?"

"I had not planned on it. I thought I would do some sketching instead."

Her mother sighed. "Not more sketching."

"You spend too much time sketching," her father said. "A young girl like you should be out and about in society."

The unspoken part of her parents' protest was *How does sketching attract a husband?* Lydia reminded them, "We are going to dine at Squire Hewitt's tomorrow night."

"His oldest son is only fourteen," her mother pointed out. "Much too young."

Exasperated, Lydia replied, "Calling on Fanny doesn't bring me to a suitor's notice either."

"It's a shame about Winterbourne's death." Her mother shook her head at the lost opportunity. "A duke would have been perfect for you."

Her father grunted. "He was a good man, too. He rode well. One of the best seats in the county."

"Not well enough," Lydia muttered under her breath.

The Duke of Winterbourne had died in a riding accident. He had been a rougher, younger version of her father. Before her Season had introduced her to other eligible men, Lydia had been perfectly content to oblige her parents' wishes and marry George. Although she loved her father, George had fallen short of her ideal husband. Now her perfect husband would be the epitome of gentlemanly behavior, refined, a courtier like the beaus who had clustered around her in London.

Lydia shrugged. She would have liked to become a duchess. George's unexpected death had sent his ward, Fanny, into a year of mourning and Lydia into a tense London Season, knowing she no longer had a backup suitor.

"You have been home for almost a sennight. It would be rude to delay calling upon Fanny much longer." Her mother eyed her with significance. "Besides, you might chance an introduction to the new duke. He is unmarried, and I believe he is in residence now."

Her mother's information was always accurate. Lydia knew when she was defeated. Her duty was clear. "I will call on Fanny tomorrow."

Satisfied, her mother took a sip of tea. "Be sure to take your maid with you when you go sketching."

"Yes, Mama."

After breakfast, Lydia gathered her pad and colored pencils. She glanced down the hall toward the small morning room where her mother met daily with the housekeeper. Meg was upstairs doing some sewing and preparing the potions necessary to maintain the fashionable style of the ladies of the house. Lydia knew she should bring the maid along for propriety's sake. It was what a dutiful daughter did.

And yet—

She obviously was not a dutiful daughter, for she was disinclined to seek Meg's company. How could she find any enjoyment in her drawing accompanied by someone whose very presence emanated disapproval? It was enough to kill any muse.

Besides, she did not intend to go very far.

Alone, Lydia slipped out of the house and moved across

the lawn until she reached the sheltering confines of the Home Wood. Once the branches, which were in the final full leaf before autumn, hid her from any view, she slowed her stride to an amble, not certain of where to go.

The excuse to sketch was merely an escape. Lydia looked down at the sketchbook and pencils she held. Drawing was one of her talents—not merely a ladylike ability. She would take deep pleasure in spending several hours creating a prettier world.

The first site she happened upon was by the small stream. She spread her blanket on a boulder. After sitting on it, she opened her pad and picked up her pencil. She glanced around, seeking inspiration. A few quick strokes and the weeping willow on the other side took shape on her paper. Yet, after a bit, she frowned. Her rendition looked like any other tree in a forest, not that particular one. She had not captured its essence. Not surprising, since she felt so out of sorts. With a sigh, she rose, gathered her supplies, and resumed her wandering.

Perhaps because the morning's conversation had involved the duke, her steps took her to the hill overlooking the grounds of Winterbourne Castle. It spread before her in all its glory. The gray stone walls absorbed the warmth of the September sun. The windows sparkled above the gardens filled with blooms of every hue. She was too far away to identify the individual flowers, but the blues, pinks, whites, and reds blossomed their beauty.

She spread her cloth beneath a tree. After a few moments to drink in the beauty, she opened her pad and began to draw. An idealized picture of the castle formed under her pencil. The strong stone walls softened as she added to the profusion of flowers until they framed her picture.

Here, alone, she found peace. It was just she and her sketchbook. Nothing would disturb her.

"If you let that north pasture lie fallow for the rest of the year and the cows continue to graze, it will be ready for seed next spring."

Listening to his cousin Cecil buzz like a pesky fly, John Penhope, the Duke of Winterbourne, was proud of his ability to withstand the urge to shoo Cecil away. The book he had been reading lay open on the desk before him. Words blurred on the page. John glanced at the book, hoping his cousin would take the hint. Yet Cecil talked and talked—and talked.

"I am not certain which crop you will prefer. I suggest you investigate to determine which one will give you the greatest yield in produce and pounds." Cecil stretched his lips to reveal his even, white teeth.

The expression denoted that his cousin had made a witticism. John smiled dutifully. Anything to send Cecil on his way so he could return to reading the biography of Alexander the Great that he had unearthed from the crowded bookshelves. One of the few benefits of inheriting the dukedom was that the library at the castle now belonged to him. He allowed the housemaids in to dust but jealously guarded the task of inventorying the books for himself.

"You are so much more knowledgeable about this than I. Why don't you investigate the crops?" John replied.

Cecil pursed his lips. "The decision should be yours. It is not my place, your grace."

"Yes, yes." John could not resist waving his hand impatiently. "I rely on your thoroughness to help me." In his few short months here as the duke, he had learned Cecil was always thorough.

His cousin considered. "Wheat could be a possibility. Or hops."

"I am certain you will determine whichever one is best." He would say anything to make Cecil leave. The biography called to him like one of the Greek sirens. Alexander the Great had been the man who conquered the known world and then cried that there were no more lands for him to claim. The author had made the long-dead hero come alive. The man's powerful character and his decisiveness fascinated John. He doubted the Greek hero would have suffered the interruption Cecil represented. Alexander had probably never had to decide which crops to plant.

"I will look into it." Cecil pulled a sheet of paper from the sheaf on the stack he carried and wrote a note. "Now I must turn your attention to the stables."

"The stables? I thought those were kept in excellent condition." The one thing John would have bet on was that his half brother had taken care of his horses.

Cecil pursed his lips again. "*I* think they are in adequate condition, but the previous duke planned some extensive renovations. The contractor submitted the plans."

"Were they approved?"

"I regret to say the previous duke met with his accident before they were finalized."

"Then there is no obligation. The stables are fine the way they are."

"I believe the man expects payment for the plans."

"Then pay him and send him away." Would this meeting ever finish? Cecil's never-ending concerns tired him. His cousin inserted his nose into every function of the estate. He was an excellent secretary.

In fact, looking at Cecil, an observer would think he was the duke. His brown hair was neatly combed, his coat tailored with a fine hand, and his cravat snowy white and crisply starched. John's own coat had been tailored for comfort while he was still a student at Oxford. With time, the cuffs had frayed, and the elbows had been patched. Appropriate attire for a scholar of the classics, not a duke. But then, he had never expected to ascend to the rank.

Even after a year, he could not believe his half brother was gone. He had never thought there was a horse George could not ride or a jump he could not take. Yet there had been one. Now the lands, the responsibilities—even his brother's name, Winterbourne—belonged to John Penhope. He did not want it. He only wanted to return to his studies. But one could not go back. There was no escaping the responsibilities of a dukedom.

Cecil's question interrupted his woolgathering. "So, your grace, what price would you prefer?"

He had no idea what his cousin was blathering about. "Surely the lowest price is preferable."

Cecil pursed his lips. John hated the action. "The lowest, your grace? Very well, although I believe sending those coal shipments to London would produce a greater profit."

"Very likely so." Apparently he was supposed to select the highest price, not the lowest. John was not going to correct his mistake, no matter how tightly Cecil pressed his lips together.

"The next matter I must discuss with your grace is—"

"That is enough for this morning." John stood.

Cecil rose slowly. "There are still—"

"No, not now." He was finished, even if Cecil was not.

"As you wish, your grace. I can discuss these matters with you later."

His cousin shuffled his papers, knocking over the small pile of invitations sitting on the corner of the desk. Impatience shot through John. "You can make some of these decisions about the estate," he said.

"These matters deserve your determination, your grace. Not mine."

In other words, John thought, *it's your place, not mine*. Aloud, he said, "Thank you for your care. I am fortunate to have you."

With a bow, Cecil left the library. At last John was alone. He restacked the invitations.

Social events were another obligation of the dukedom— and one he dreaded. When he was a student, talking to women, especially young unmarried ones, left him with sweating palms and stuttering speech. They always seemed to speak in a language he did not understand. It sounded like English, but the underlying meanings escaped him. But now he understood the ladies' goal. A single duke needed a duchess. It was another responsibility he had inherited.

Scowling, he put that thought out of his mind. He sat on his chair and pulled the biography forward, ready to resume his favorite pastime. He found the spot where he had been when his cousin interrupted him and began to read.

After a moment he shifted on his seat into a more comfortable position. When that did not bring back the magic produced by the author's words, he stretched his neck and rolled his shoulders—something Cecil could never do in his close-fitting jacket. That thought reminded him his cousin was the one who had broken the spell.

He frowned. He wanted to retreat into the world of ancient Greece. He wanted to live through Alexander the Great's conquest of Persia. And he could not. Even though his cousin was gone, his influence still interfered with the contemplative mood John sought. He would not recapture that peaceful haven anytime soon.

With a snort of disgust, he stood. He had to escape from the walls of this place. Even his beloved library offered no refuge. He was the Duke of Winterbourne. Every stone, every brick, even every candlestick, belonged to him. He owned it all, and the weight crushed him.

To avoid the front hall and his butler, Scott, he went out through the library doors. They opened onto the stone terrace fronting the house. John leapt over the balustrade like a schoolboy and raced into the woods.

He was huffing when he leaned against the tree, both from laughter and the speed of his run. He was free.

He looked back at the castle. It loomed above him as if to say, "You cannot escape."

It was true. He could not escape forever. This freedom was only temporary. He would have to return. He must.

His laughter stopped. Straightening, he brushed the bark from his shoulders. He turned his back on the castle and sauntered away among the trees. For a little while, he would forget the dukedom and all its obligations. Determined to savor every sensation, he filled his lungs with the heavy summer air, redolent with the scent of the woods. Last year's leaves provided a thick carpet beneath his boots. In the heat of the day, the buzz of insects was faint, punctured by the occasional outburst of a songbird.

The pace of his stride slowed when he began to climb the slight rise. Once on the other side, he would not be able to catch a glimpse of Winterbourne Castle.

The longer he walked, the heavier his coat became. A true gentleman should not be seen in his shirtsleeves, but John was tired of the strictures. Besides, what was the sense of being a duke if one could not do as one pleased? After all, only royalty outranked him. He stripped off the coat and slung it over his shoulders.

His back straightened and his shoulders squared. A feeling of peace permeated his being. He could feel the wrinkles in his spirit being ironed away by the woods drowsing in the heat. Perhaps he would make such a walk a part of his daily routine. If he had known how to whistle, he would have done so.

Strolling along completely at one with his world, he rounded a large oak and stopped, stunned. Someone was seated in his path.

"What are you doing here?" he asked, irritated that even when escaping he could not be alone.

"Oh!" The young woman scrambled to her feet, scattering art supplies willy-nilly.

Her gaze lifted to his, and he realized he had never seen eyes quite that shade of blue before. Beneath her wide straw hat, golden ringlets framed a visage that could have belonged to Aphrodite, or perhaps Helen of Troy, she whose face had launched a thousand ships.

John started to whip his hat from his head and then remembered he had not put one on. "Forgive me. I did not mean to startle you."

"I know I should not be here, but please do not tattle on me."

She smiled at him, and he knew hot pokers would not cause him to reveal her presence.

"I should not be here either," he said.

"Then our secrets are mutually safe."

He glanced around. "What about your maid?"

"She is one of those I am hiding from."

She was escaping, too. He liked her already. "It could be dangerous out here alone."

Her smile wavered. "Are you trying to frighten me?"

"No." He did not want her to run off and vanish like a forest nymph. Before his inheritance, experience had taught him women left his presence as quickly as they could. "Just being careful."

"There is nothing to fear around here. These woods belong to Winterbourne."

"Belonging to a duke makes the place safe?"

She laughed, and he liked her even more. Obviously she did not recognize him. Encouraged by her acceptance, he asked again in a politer tone, "What are you doing here?"

"I was sketching the castle."

"May I see?"

"Certainly." She picked up the sketchbook she had dropped.

Her drawing showed a vision of the castle as he had never seen it. Broad leaves wreathed the paper, giving the viewer the impression of peering through a bush. Flowers spread over the ground around the castle, making it appear to float on a cloud of blossoms. Behind it, the sun's rays shone, as if it were in the act of rising or setting.

"That's not possible," John said.

"What?"

"The sun cannot be in back of the castle. This view of it is the southern side."

"So?"

"The sun rises in the east and sets in the west."

She widened her eyes. Her eyelashes were thick and golden.

"I know that," she said. "This is just a picture. It's not real."

Her laughter invited him to join in. Of course, he knew the picture was not real. Laughing, he marveled at the ease with which he was conversing with a beautiful girl. He did not want to lose her friendly air.

To make amends for his criticism, he said, "You draw very well."

"Thank you, kind sir." She cocked her head at him, merriment alive in the twinkle in her eyes and the curve of her lips. "I can't keep calling you 'sir.' Who are you?"

"My name is Alexander," John lied.

Chapter Two

Lydia knew there was something wrong with his answer, but she could not put her finger on what exactly troubled her. "Are you Mr. Alexander or is that your Christian name?"

His gaze fell away from hers. "My first name. My surname is Penhope."

"You must be Fanny's cousin." At his nod, she said, "Since she is not here to introduce us, she will have to act as our absent presenter. I am her friend Lydia Grenville."

He bowed. "I appreciate Fanny's assistance."

"Yes." She smiled with mischief. "The best kind of help is rendered when the giver is absent."

There was no responding sally. Instead, he seemed to consider her remark. He puzzled her. He wore his dark hair simply dressed and without a hat, a sign of low rank. His coat cuffs were fraying, yet the quality of the cloth could not be denied. Fanny had mentioned a cousin who worked for the new duke. Because of his fair skin, Lydia surmised that this man must spend most of his time working indoors. Perhaps he was a representative of a poorer branch of the Penhope family. Was he the secretary? Had he slipped out for a momentary escape?

"What are you hiding from?" she asked, determined to ferret out his social status through conversation.

His lips twisted into a grimace. "It is my duty to care for the estates."

The secretary, just as she had assumed. She tamped down her disappointment. Her momentary interest in him could not be allowed to blossom. What a shame. She said, "That's an important position. Everyone must depend upon you."

"Yes, everyone." His flat statement held a bucketful of bitterness.

She struggled to lighten his mood. "But now—here—no one depends upon you. There are no demands."

"They still exist. I cannot escape them."

She wanted to see him smile. With his hazel eyes and lean face, he was a fine-looking man. He would be handsome if happiness but animated his features. She set herself to charm him. "Not here. Your duties cannot follow you into these woods."

"Are you some kind of fairy who can make troubles disappear?"

"Of course." She picked up her pencil and waved it as though casting a spell. "I hereby banish all difficulties and problems from this place." Turning back to him, she said, "Now nothing can mar your peace."

As though to test her assertion, he took a deep breath and held it before releasing it with a sigh. "You are a lady of magic."

His smile started in the center of his lips and spread to the corners. The merriment in his eyes began like the flicker of a candle catching on the wick, then glowing into a steady light. She was right. He was a very handsome man, and she enjoyed the company of such men.

She sat down and arranged her skirt becomingly before patting the cloth. "You may sit here."

He hesitated. "Beside you?"

"Of course." He was shy. She found the trait endearing. So many men snatched at every bit of concession and demanded more. "I am the fairy princess. No troubles will intrude."

With careful movements, he settled himself at the edge of the cloth. His long legs stretched out before him. They were well shaped, with no need of padding to pretend at musculature that did not exist. His shoes were scuffed, likely from hiking in the woods.

She liked him—nothing more. He did not mock her whimsical play, but accepted it in a respectful fashion. She wanted to study him more closely. Apparently a shy man, he would not like being the focus of her attention. Resolutely, she turned her sketchpad to a fresh page.

"What will you draw?" he asked.

"I have already done the castle." She glanced around, seeking a subject for inspiration. Her gaze took in the trees and the interesting patterns formed by the fallen branches, but it was he who attracted her eyes. She wrenched her head away. He would not be a proper subject. "Shall I let you choose?"

"Me? I'm not an artist."

"You are in an enchanted forest, sir. You've been conversing with the fairy princess, a privilege not granted to many. Now I grant you a greater honor. Whatever you pick, I will sketch." She smiled at him, but there was a challenge in her words.

His eyes widened slightly, but he did not reject her dare. His head turned as he considered several options. She thought he might take the obvious choice of the bunch of white wildflowers clustered beneath an oak tree. They were the conventional pretty picture.

"What about there?" He pointed a little to her left.

She looked but did not see what he meant. "Do you mean that tree with the broken branch?" It was not too challenging, but maybe he had selected the subject out of desperation.

"No, I meant its roots. Do you see how they form triangles intersecting with triangles?"

She saw. The tree roots poked through the dirt at odd angles before plunging underground again. Others overlaid them, weaving an intricate pattern. She slid a curious glance at him. "You have a good eye to spot something like that."

He shifted under her praise. She understood. With his position in the ducal household, his talents were probably not much complimented.

"Do you study art?" she asked.

"Only that of ancient Greece. Everything about that era fascinates me."

"I know little about that time."

"The Greeks believed in symmetry in their art. They tried to apply order to everything in their lives: architecture, science, government. Did you know that many of our mathematical principles were laid down by them?"

"No, I did not." It was such an odd topic, but his enthusiasm caught her interest. No one had ever talked about mathematics to her. Usually she heard only praises of her beauty. He was different, and he intrigued her.

"Thalus is truly the father of much Greek thought. He lived in Ionia, and he tried to analyze nature's laws through observation. If he could understand the principle behind how nature worked, then things would not be left to chance. Have you heard of Thalus?" Animation lit his whole body.

When she shook her head, he continued. "He is ranked as

one of the seven great wise men of antiquity. He determined which stars sailors could use in navigation. He invented calculations to determine the size of a farmer's field."

"Why is that so important?" Lydia asked.

"If the farmer knows how big the field is, he can determine how much seed he needs and how much yield that seed is producing." Alexander pulled his knees up and clasped his arms around them. "Thalus used the results from what he witnessed to develop his theories. His approach inspired mathematics and the logic of the philosophers. It even led to the beginning of medicine by relying on observation for cures instead of magic."

Awe filled Lydia. "One man did all that?"

"He was not the only great man." He leaned forward. "Greece was the beginning of our civilization. There were many great men then. Men such as Plato, Socrates, Pericles, and Alexander."

"That's your name, too," she said. This man knew so much and shared it in such an eager manner that she wanted to learn more. "What did he do?"

He looked away, probably shy again now that she had interrupted him. She regretted snipping the conversational bond too soon.

"Tell me about him," she coaxed.

Her encouragement worked. "Alexander the Great was a tremendous warrior. He tried to model himself on Homer's Achilles, who took as his motto 'Ever to be the best.' Using that as his guide, Alexander conquered the entire world."

"All of it?"

"What was known at that time, yes. His empire stretched from Egypt to India, but it did not last beyond his death. The generals who inherited it could fight but not govern."

"Naturally," Lydia said.

He raised an eyebrow. "'Naturally?' What do you mean?"

"They were generals and trained for war. Governing is a very different discipline."

"Do they not both require men to take command?"

"Yes, but men of a different temperament and talent." The one thing she had studied diligently was men and how they thought.

For a moment he mulled over her statement. "Would you not say that for men to command an army or to govern, decisive leadership is required?"

She nodded. "Yes, decisive, but different dispositions."

"What do you mean?" he asked with genuine interest.

Encouraged, she remembered some of the military men who'd partnered her at dinner parties. "I would think a successful general would be a man able to adapt quickly to fast-moving changes, yet always keeping his eye on the purpose of winning the battle."

"And a man for governing?"

"He has more time and can consider how to solve a problem. He can seek advice from others before he makes his decisions."

"An analytical man," he mused. "That is an interesting point of view. I had not considered that. Very good, Miss Grenville."

At his compliment, she tingled with delight from her hair to her toes. Never before had an opinion of hers been considered worthy of notice. Yet this man did not brush her idea aside; he discussed it with her. She studied him more closely, observing his straight nose and firm chin. Brown lashes surrounded his hazel eyes, and at the corners there were very faint squint lines, as if he spent much time reading by candlelight.

He studied her, too, she saw. For the first time, shyness

filled her. Many men had praised her beauty. Did her looks attract him, too? She gave herself a mental shake. What a silly notion! As if she should care what a secretary thought.

"I am not making much progress on your picture." Lydia lifted the blank page for his perusal.

"I can wait."

"Will you not be missed?"

Another slow smile. This man did everything in a deliberate fashion. It had her breathless with anticipation for the result, to see how handsome he was and to feel that bond of merriment forming again. When his smile appeared, it was well worth the wait.

"Most likely," he said. "After all, who else can do what I do?"

"Indeed." She knew a good secretary would make one's life so much easier. Such a servant could not easily be replaced.

"And you? Will you not be missed?" he asked.

She glanced at the sun, which was high in the sky. Trepidation spiked within her. "Do you know the time?"

He pulled out a plain gold pocket watch. "It is a quarter past one."

"Oh, no!" She scrambled to her feet. "I have missed luncheon. My mother will be vexed."

He rose and picked up her sketchbook and pencils. He held them out to her. The page was still blank.

Taking them from him, she said, "I am sorry. I did not draw your roots. I wanted to."

"Will you do it for me on the morrow?"

"Tomorrow?"

The brightness in his face faded. "Of course, you have other commitments."

A failed debutante was never truly wanted nearby. Her

bad luck might rub off on someone. "No, I am free. I will draw it for you tomorrow."

He held out his arm. "May I escort you home?"

"Do you know where I live?"

"Grenville Manor," he guessed, with a twinkle in his eye.

"Correct." She laughed. "That wasn't too difficult to determine, was it?"

She placed her hand on his arm and went with him through the woods bursting with the end-of-season bounty. Hidden among the oak branches, the birds sang their choruses. A white butterfly flitted across their path. The slight breeze prevented the sun's beams from being too hot.

It was a pleasurable stroll, but Lydia did not dare let anyone know she had met a man in the woods—even if he was a perfect gentleman. She must protect her reputation in hope for her future. Her trepidation grew to apprehension.

At the edge of the trees, she halted him. "I can go on from here—alone."

"It is not much farther."

"No, but it would not be wise."

With a glance at the manor, he understood. He dropped his arm. "Of course. I must not be seen. I will watch your safe arrival from here."

"Thank you, Mr. Penhope."

She curtseyed and turned for home. After a couple of steps, she glanced back. A tree hid his body, but his head peered around the trunk, just as in a game of hide-and-seek.

"I will get my picture tomorrow?" he called.

"Most assuredly, sir."

Hurrying for home, she knew she faced a scolding from her mother for vanishing for so long. Yet the prospect did not rattle Lydia. She had something to look forward to.

Her foot slipped suddenly on a bump, and she glanced

back. In the shade of the trees, she could not spot Alexander's face, but she knew he still watched. Her heart quickened its beat. She had made a secret assignation with a man she had just met. Her deed flew in the face of every rule of good behavior. How easy it had been to abandon every one of those rules that had been drilled into her since childhood. They should be part of her very nature.

Secret meetings, if they became known, would cast such a stain on her reputation that it could never be cleansed. Despite her adequate dowry, her reputation was her major asset for attracting an appropriate suitor. She would have to be careful.

Even so, she would not go back and tell him not to expect her. Her mother already waited and worried.

Lydia would only fulfill her promise to draw one picture for him. Then she would leave. No matter how flattered she was by his compliments on her opinion, she could never accept the attentions of a ducal secretary. She was destined for a grander match.

"Fool!" John called himself as he watched her cross the lawn and enter the front door. "Idiot!" His hand clenched into a fist. He felt the bark scrape against his fingers, recalling him to where he was—in the Home Wood just east of Grenville Manor.

He could not stay here. He must return to Winterbourne Castle. What if someone spotted him skulking in the forest as if he were a poacher? Their puzzlement at his sneaking manner would be nothing compared to their laughter at the predicament he had created for himself.

Shaking his head, he began to walk home. A large pinecone lay in his path. He kicked it and heard it thump against a tree. The gesture did not relieve his frustration.

Why had he told her his name was Alexander? What fit of madness had possessed him?

He must reason this out. Maybe then he would understand his actions. Maybe then he could save himself future humiliation when his deception was revealed—as it surely would be.

One, he had escaped the castle, driven from it by Cecil's demands on his attention. Two, he had entered the woods, where no one expected anything of him. And three, he had met the most beautiful girl in the world.

Women always addled his wits. He never knew what to say to them. As a scholar he had been able to escape any social duties by turning to his studies.

Miss Grenville's presence had surprised him. He'd had no time to think before she was asking who he was. He knew where the "Alexander" had come from—that biography he still wanted to read.

Could he go back and hide between its pages? Pretend this meeting never happened?

Of course not.

He was the Duke of Winterbourne. Sooner or later, he and Miss Grenville would meet. The local society was not that large. She would learn he had deceived her, and she would wonder why.

He groaned and clutched his hair. How could he explain that she made him so at ease? He had no difficulty in talking with her. The first thing that popped into his head jumped off his tongue. Her interest was no act, even when he talked about ancient Greeks and mathematics. What other woman was like that? None, as he knew from bitter experience.

She had not even known he was a duke. There was no deceit in her friendliness.

But someday his rank would be revealed.

He took a deep breath. Tomorrow, when he met with her, he would have to tell the truth. He must confess. It was the only way to minimize the future embarrassment. Of course, once he did, she would never again treat him with so much ease. No woman ever did with a duke.

The next morning, Lydia woke with anticipation whipping through her like a strong summer wind. Yesterday she had endured the expected scolding from her mother and had accepted it meekly. It was deserved.

But that was yesterday. Today was a clean start, full of promise. She was going to slip away to the woods surrounding Winterbourne Castle and sketch that grouping of roots. It was important that she do so. She had promised. Not even the prospect of another scolding from her mother would deter her. After all, today Lydia would watch the time. Her mother wouldn't even notice she was missing.

Nothing could mar Lydia's excitement. Not even when her maid pulled her hair while dressing it.

"Sorry, miss," Meg said through the comb clenched between her teeth. Each of her hands held a lock of Lydia's hair.

Lydia did not snap at her. "It doesn't matter. Just do your best work."

"Yes, miss."

In the looking glass, Lydia could see surprise spark in her maid's eyes. Best work was usually requested only when an important social occasion warranted it. There had been such activities every night in London. Life at Grenville Manor was much quieter.

To allay Meg's curiosity, Lydia said, "Just because I am back home is no reason to reduce the standards of dress."

"Yes, miss."

"After all, one never knows who one might meet." Lydia stilled her reckless tongue, too late. She did not mean to keep Meg's interest in her mistress's day alive.

"Perhaps you would prefer your blue dress for today instead?" The pale green one currently lay on the bed.

"No, the green one will be fine." Lydia had selected it because she hoped to remind Alexander Penhope of a forest fairy princess. If she dared, she would put some of those white wildflowers in her hair. As it was, she said, "I will want the bonnet with the white flowers and green ribbons."

Even in the woods, Lydia would be mindful to protect her complexion from the sun's harmful rays. She sat still, watching in the looking glass while Meg finished fixing her hair. The result pleased Lydia. Her hair was pulled back, cascading down the nape of her neck in a waterfall of curls. Its very simplicity was a testament to her maid's skill.

"Very good, Meg."

"Thank you, miss."

Meg stepped away to get the bonnet, while Lydia stood beside the dress on the bed. The maid pulled the hatbox down from the armoire shelf and lifted out the bonnet to set it beside the dress.

As Lydia watched Meg, it occurred to her that the other woman was in her mid-twenties. Lydia's goal in life was a successful marriage. Did Meg have any dreams? What did a lady's maid hope for in life? Such a thought had never crossed Lydia's mind before, but having talked so freely with a secretary yesterday opened her eyes to those of the lower class surrounding her.

Meg was just Meg—always there—a stout maid in a serviceable dress, whose dark brown hair was properly worn in a neat bun. Maybe Lydia's plans for the day caused her to wonder about the other girl's secrets—had Meg ever slipped out of the manor for a clandestine meeting with a man?

Lydia took off her wrapper. Meg laid it on the bed and lifted the green dress over her mistress's head. While enveloped in the fabric, Lydia could not see the maid's face. It was easier to ask, "Meg, have you ever had a suitor?"

Meg's hands stilled. "A suitor, miss? Me? Why do you ask?"

The maid had not denied it outright. Surprised, Lydia realized Meg had a beau right now. Her head poked through the dress's neckline. "Who is he?"

"He, miss?" Her maid busied herself with tugging the folds of the dress into place.

"Come, you don't need to pretend with me. Tell me about him."

Meg eyed her suspiciously. Both of them knew a maid should have no other concerns but her mistress's comfort.

"I am interested," Lydia coaxed. "What is his name?"

Meg clutched the dress fabric so tightly her grip probably left wrinkles. "Ben, miss. He works at the inn, in the stables."

"The stables? Meg, you are a lady's maid."

Pride lifted the girl's chin. "Ben's ambitious, miss. He's the head groom, and he's going to have his own inn someday."

Being an innkeeper was much more respectable than just working as a stable hand. There was a great social gulf between being an owner and being a worker.

"When do you think he will achieve this?" Lydia asked.

"Not for another year or so. Ben's saving his money. He's careful, and he's smart." Meg tied the dress closures in the back for Lydia. "Don't worry, Miss Lydia. I'll be around until you wed."

"Thank you." Lydia's smile stiffened on her face. She did

not like Meg's implication that it could take another year or more to see her wed—even if it was the truth.

Breakfast was no easier.

"No," her mother said. "No sketching. I do not want to worry about you as I did yesterday."

"Mother, please. I will keep better watch on the time."

In her mother's irritation, the muffin crumbled between her fingers. "Why is it so important that you sketch in the woods today? You can stay in the garden instead."

Lydia dared not reveal the true reason. "I did not finish my picture yesterday."

"I think calling on Fanny is far more important. I have ordered the carriage readied for you. Now that her year of mourning is over, it would be quite proper to invite her for dinner. The night after tomorrow would be perfect." Her mother gave her a significant glance. "Include the new duke in the invitation."

"Yes, Mother."

There would be no escaping a call on Fanny this morning. Maybe this afternoon she could slip away. She would be too late to meet Mr. Penhope, but she would keep her promise to draw for him.

Fanny welcomed her with open arms, eager to dissect Lydia's Season. "Since we were not able to share it together, you must make me feel as though I was there. Nothing ever happens around here."

The girls sat on a couch in the small yellow and white morning room Fanny had claimed for her own use. She was in her mid-twenties, only a year older than Lydia, with cropped brown curls and a sharp face. Today she wore a lavender dress with ribbon trim at the sleeves and flounces.

Lydia tried to convey the Season's excitement, but it was

not easy to make events sound like triumphs when they both knew the final outcome was a failure.

Fanny patted her friend's arm. "Maybe next year we can go to London together."

"I hope so," Lydia said. She did not reveal her hidden fear that one Season was all her father would pay for. Of course, she was his treasured poppet, but would he regard the expense of another Season as good money chasing after bad? Suitors were within reach in the surrounding countryside, even if she did not prefer them. After all, there was an available duke lurking in these very halls. Unfortunately the only one who interested her was Mr. Alexander Penhope—and he was just a secretary. Not a suitable candidate. Lydia knew her duty.

"Mother wanted me to ask you and his grace to dinner for the night after next. It would be an opportunity for us to welcome him to the neighborhood."

"Yes, Winterbourne did not arrive at the castle until after you had left for London." Fanny made a moue of distaste. "He wanted to complete his classes at Oxford."

"He must be very intelligent."

"He spends much of his time shut in his library. He is so caught up in his ancient Greeks, I don't think he knows he lives in Essex." Fanny warned, "You will not like him."

It did not matter if Lydia liked him—he was an unmarried duke. "Then he needs to get outside more. Perhaps I can induce him to show me the delights of our countryside." Tilting her head, she smiled her most enticing smile. She knew she made a charming picture.

The image did not impress Fanny. "Good luck," she said glumly. "He's not like George. It's hard to believe they were brothers. John has spent his whole life surrounded by books. Even when he lived here as a boy, he chose to spend his time with his tutor. George would be forever in the stables or tearing up the countryside. John never ventured out. I doubt he knows how to treat a woman, unless she is a statue carved out of marble and is missing her arms."

"All men will respond to a pretty woman. It's part of their nature." Lydia was determined not to be so exacting in her standards when luring a duke. She'd made her mistake in London. Duty, not desire, was now her guide.

Fanny shook her head. "Not Winterbourne. When he first came to the castle, many of the ladies made condolence calls, bringing their daughters along, of course."

"Of course." The competition did not daunt Lydia.

"It was no use. When Elizabeth Chandler called, Winterbourne sat in his chair, sipping his tea and barely participating in any conversation."

"No surprise. She handles both sides of a conversation quite adequately by herself."

"He did not talk to Mary Fisher, either, and you know how quiet she is."

"She would not say boo if a mouse ran up her skirts. If he is a shy man, he needs some conversational help to begin." Lydia smoothed her dress. "Ancient Greeks seem like just the place to start."

"What do you know of ancient Greeks?"

Lydia tossed her head so her carefully arranged curls danced. "You would be surprised. For instance, I know Thalus was the father to many of the sciences we use today."

The shock on Fanny's face pleased Lydia.

"Where did you learn that?" her friend demanded.

That she had no intention of revealing. She contented herself with looking serious. "Did you know that Alexander the Great conquered the entire known world? He was the

Napoleon of his time. The empire fell apart after Alexander's death because his generals couldn't govern."

"Maybe you *will* be able to talk to Winterbourne," Fanny said slowly. "You sound just like him. I know that Cecil and I can get nothing else out of him."

At the new name, Lydia's interest quickened. "Who is Cecil?"

"I don't think you've met him. He is our cousin who works for Winterbourne as his secretary."

"Oh?" Her heart beat a little faster.

"Cecil has many ideas for improving the estates, such as crop rotation, but Winterbourne never listens to him."

"It must frustrate him to be ignored."

"Winterbourne ignores everyone, which may be for the best. If he never marries and does not beget an heir, then Cecil is next in line for the title. He would implement all kinds of modern ideas." Fanny sighed. "Life never does work out correctly."

"Indeed," Lydia said, but her mind was elsewhere, scrambling to figure out this new information. Now she understood Alexander's need to escape yesterday. Something must have been the straw that broke his patience with the duke. Perhaps one more idea shoved aside. "I would like to meet him. Please invite him to the dinner, too."

She hugged this new knowledge to herself. She knew Alexander's identity. She even sympathized with why he was in the woods—and she would tax him with it the next time she met him.

During the drive home from her morning call on Fanny, Lydia wondered when she would again see Alexander—or Cecil, as he was named. Yesterday their meeting had been accidental. She had promised to draw his picture of roots, and she meant to do that. Today, if at all possible. Even if he would not be there, she intended to slip out this afternoon, after reassuring her mother with an appearance at the luncheon table.

Yet, as she shut the side door to the manor behind her and headed toward the Home Wood, a secret part within her hoped she might see him today. This time there was no wandering from site to site. She knew where to go.

Once in the clearing, she spread her blanket and sat. Placing her pencils just so and opening her sketchbook, she hugged to herself the knowledge of who and what he was. Her suspicions had been confirmed.

The woods drowsed in the heat of midday. The birds were quiet, and only an occasional breeze stirred the sleepy atmosphere.

Lydia was not sleepy. Her eyes were wide and alert, and her heart beat with anticipation, even as her fingers stroked the roots' pattern into existence on her paper. Despite her immersion in her work, her hearing remained acute. After a time, the snap of a twig and the rustle of leaves underfoot announced the approach of someone else.

She turned her head, and delight curved her lips when she spotted "Alexander" Penhope.

"Good afternoon," he said with a bow.

"Good afternoon," she replied. "I know who you are."

Chapter Three

*F*lames of embarrassment flared down John's spine at
Lydia's words. She knew who he was. Deluded fool.
He should have told her immediately. He should never have
begun this silly deception. Now it was too late.

"I can explain," he began, already knowing he had no explanation.

She laughed. "There is no need. I understand."

"You do?"

"Yes. Your name is Cecil Penhope, and you are Winterbourne's secretary."

He stared at her. "How did you come to that conclusion?"

"It was not hard. I called upon Fanny this morning."

He knew about her visit because he had overheard her
speaking when he had passed in the hall. He had paused outside the door, debating. Should he enter? As much as he
wanted to see Lydia again, he knew that if he went into the
drawing room, his deception would be immediately revealed.
Fanny's greeting would give him away.

Courage had deserted him. He had walked away, epithets
echoing in his mind. Now, through her misunderstanding, he
had once again escaped an unmasking. She thought he was
Cecil. This was even worse. He must correct her. He must re-

veal his identity. But once she knew, their easy friendship would shatter, and he would be locked behind the barrier of his rank.

He did not meet her eyes. "I must tell you, I know the deception was wrong. I should never even have begun it."

She laid a gentle hand upon his arm. Although her touch was light, every nerve in his body suddenly focused upon that limb.

"Cecil or Alexander, it matters not, for I still must call you Mr. Penhope," she said.

Actually, she should call him "your grace," but looking at her hand against his coat sleeve, he lacked the courage to tell her that. He grasped at the chance to enjoy her company for a little while longer. "I do like the name Alexander."

"It is a noble name."

He continued to gaze at where she touched him. She wore no glove, having removed it while she sketched. Her skin was soft and white against the rough fabric of his coat. Her fingers were slender, the nails well formed. A black smudge darkened the side of her ring finger. It seemed so endearing to notice that one imperfection. Despite her beauty, which awed him, she was not a perfect being. The realization gave him a small bit of courage.

"What are you sketching?" he asked.

She withdrew her hand to pick up the pad. A pang of regret shot through him at the loss of her touch.

"The picture you suggested."

"I suggested?"

"Yes, the roots. Remember?"

He did now. "Of course."

"To my surprise, it is actually an interesting study in perspective. The triangles form patterns on top of patterns. See?"

She held out the sketchbook. He saw the patterns she spoke of. Triangles intersected with other triangles, some upside down and smaller ones formed inside bigger ones.

"This is quite impressive," he said. "You did a study of basic shapes in something ordinarily overlooked."

A pinkening of her cheeks rewarded his compliment, and a wave of pleasure flushed through him.

"You are most kind," she said.

"I am trying to be honest."

"The truth is not something I often hear from a man."

She gazed straight into his eyes. He could not look away, even if he had wished to do so. Her eyes were a true blue, the color of the sky and clear as a lake. With all his education, he should be able to conjure up better comparisons, but he had never before needed to think of how to describe a lady's charms. He had never paid attention to poetry, unless Homer wrote it. Now he wished he possessed the conversational skill expected by society's ladies.

"Forgive me, but I do not know how to offer the praises you deserve," he said.

She laughed, a merry sound that included him in her enjoyment. "I hear too many compliments, most of them false. The truth is far more rare."

The truth. Her words stung. Everything she knew about him was a lie. He must not allow her misconception to continue.

He cleared his throat. "There is something you should know."

Her merriment did not end. "Don't sound so serious."

"This is important."

Her smile remained, but some of the lightness of her manner dimmed. "Very well, then. Sit down while you tell me." She gracefully sat again on the blanket. When he did not immediately follow, she patted the spot beside her. "Come. We have both escaped—even if only temporarily. Let's not allow outside concerns to trouble us here."

He could not resist her invitation and carefully lowered himself beside her. He looked around. The oak trees stood straight like the pictures he had seen of the pillars in the Acropolis of Athens. From his position on the ground, they appeared to touch the sky. The leafy branches acted like the cornices of the Ionic columns, adding to the serene sense of being in a temple. He picked up a twig to twirl between his fingers, putting off the confession he must make. "I have come to think of this clearing as a refuge."

"Exactly. Here we can both hide from the duties others demand of us."

"You are a beautiful young lady. What duties could you have?"

She wagged a finger at him in mock admonishment. "Don't you start with that empty flattery now. It makes you sound like all the other London beaus."

No one had ever compared him to a London beau before, except in derision. Filled with daring, he said, "You are a beautiful lady. An ornament gracing wherever you pass."

"An ornament. That's flattery." She sighed. "Perhaps I wish it were so. Would life be easier then?"

"What makes your life so hard?"

"You would not understand."

"Give me a chance."

She glanced at him from under the brim of her bonnet, studying him. He hoped that his face reflected his concern. Dissembling was another social skill he lacked.

Whatever she saw seemed to reassure her, for she sighed again. "I do not like admitting this, but I failed at my primary duty to my family."

"Impossible! I do not believe it."

Her smile was a little shaky. "I appreciate your faith in me, but it is true."

The brightness had gone from her eyes as if extinguished by a candlesnuffer. Her musings pained her, and he could not bear for her to carry them alone. Tossing aside the twig, he asked, "What happened?"

She took a deep breath. "I did not marry successfully."

"I thought you were unmarried. Aren't you *Miss* Grenville?"

"Of course. That is the whole point. I am still Miss Grenville. My family paid for a London Season, and I could not snare a husband."

"The men in London are a bunch of idiots. I know they possess no brains, but are they blind as well?"

"Oh, I had offers. Just not ones I wanted to accept." She looked off into the distance for a moment, but he knew she was not seeing the trees. "The easiest to refuse were the gazetted fortune hunters. But to reject an unexceptional titled gentleman . . ." As her voice trailed off, she shook her head.

"Why refuse the titled ones?" He was curious—strictly from the viewpoint of a scholar.

"Perhaps because they were unexceptional." She shrugged. "There were only two of those. First there was a baronet. I suppose he would have been acceptable, but he offered at the beginning of the Season. I still anticipated a brilliant match. Nothing lower than an earl. I was a foolish girl, and it was a foolish rejection. An earl did propose in July at the end of the Season, but I rejected him." She shuddered. "He was so old and heavy. His corsets creaked whenever he moved. I would have been his third wife." She paused again. "I would like to claim at least affection, if not love, in my marriage."

"You did the right thing," he declared. "How can you wed without love, let alone affection? No one has the right to expect such from you."

"My dear Mr. Penhope." Once again she laid her hand upon his sleeve, causing a tingle to radiate up his arm and throughout his body. "You are a sweet and kind man to champion my cause thus, but a good marriage is my purpose in life."

Bitterness shot through him at her praise. He told her, "I am not the type of man you named me. In fact, you know nothing about me." His own perception of himself was clear. He was a deceiver, a liar, a coward afraid to face the consequences of his deception.

"Perhaps," she said, "but I think I can trust you. After all, you are a gentleman. You have proved as much during our meetings."

The sense of refuge that had permeated the clearing before vanished. He had to tell her. He must let her know who he truly was.

He cleared his throat. "Miss Grenville, there is something I must say."

"Yes?"

She turned those beautiful blue eyes toward him. They looked straight at him, without wavering, without deceit. She trusted and accepted him. She did not regard him as a bore. Her acceptance of him was too novel an experience and too pleasant for him to destroy. He could not speak the words of confession.

He glanced down at his hands. "What will you take for your next subject?"

"That is what you wanted to say?"

Hearing the bewilderment in her voice, he inwardly

mocked himself. *Coward. You call yourself Alexander, but you lack his heroic traits.*

He did not face her. After a pause, she said, "What subject do you suggest?"

In order not to look at her, he let his gaze wander around the clearing. Nothing appealed to him. His shame burned so strongly within that he wondered she did not notice its flames. "It is your turn to choose," he said gruffly.

His roughness did not put her off. "Since I usually sketch by myself, I end up choosing what to draw."

"Alone? You come out here alone?" Concern for her safety jumped within him. He had thought their initial meeting, with her alone, was a one-time occurrence, not a regular one.

"Drawing is not an activity that encourages companionship," she said.

"But you should at least have a maid!"

"Oh, pooh!" Her face took on a mischievous cast. "Have you forgotten? I am the fairy princess. These woods are my domain."

"Yes, I know." Indeed, her desire for privacy, which he understood, and her whimsical fun, which he joined in, made their meetings possible, yet their very isolation made them scandalous as well—not that the presence of a maid would mitigate the scandal much.

"Besides," Lydia said, "Meg has better things to do than follow me around when I am sketching."

"Care of her mistress should be her most important concern."

"This mistress is perfectly safe. I go only as far as my feet will take me, and I return home before I am missed."

"This is Winterbourne property," he pointed out. "Anyone

can pass through it or through the manor's lands. Who knows what kind of person you could encounter?"

"I met you, did I not? And you are a perfectly lovely person. So it all turned out for the best." With a determined set to her shoulders, she turned her attention back to the sketchbook balanced on her knees. Yet the page remained blank.

"What if you are discovered slipping out alone?"

"I have already endured one scold from my mother. If I return in time for tea, which I will, no one will know."

He glanced around. The clearing was darkening as the shadows cast by the oak trees lengthened. "What time does your family take tea?"

She followed his gaze. "Oh, no! I am late." She scrambled to her feet, scattering her book and pencils.

"Let me help you." Bending, he gathered the pencils and picked up the sketchbook.

She snatched up the blanket and clutched it close. "I'm going to be scolded again. I just know it."

He handed her the art supplies. "I will escort you."

"Only to the edge of the woods."

He agreed. She should not be discovered alone in his company.

They took off at a quick pace. Neither spoke until they reached the end of the trees. The hard walk flushed her face and caused her breasts to rise and fall noticeably. He regretted her departure.

John grabbed her hand. "I am sorry you are going to be scolded."

"I should be used to it, but I am not. I will probably be confined to the manor." She started off across the lawn surrounding the manor and then called back, "I will come back to sketch. I won't be confined forever."

She hurried to the manor, and John watched her enter

through the front door. There would be no overlooking her lateness by that route. She had the courage to face the consequences of her actions. He should do the same.

He strolled back to the castle. Copying Lydia, he entered through the main door, opening it to the surprise of his butler, Scott.

The man stiffened and then hurried to hold the door open. "Your Grace, I had not realized you had gone out."

"No need to worry. You did not know. I went out on my own."

"Of course, your grace."

Scott bowed his head as John ambled down the hall. Now that his encounter with Lydia was over, his mood darkened. He felt so at ease in her presence. It was unique to be able to chat with a beautiful woman and not worry about which word to use. Yet he had not acquitted himself well. Alexander the Great had conquered the world in an effort to be the best, while he could not even reveal his true identity to the fairy princess.

Since it was teatime, he joined Fanny and Cecil in the small drawing room. The tray with its stack of delicacies already sat before the two of them.

Fanny paused in passing a teacup to Cecil. "Winterbourne! We had not expected you."

He was surprising everyone today and relished being unexpected. He sat and reached for a biscuit. "I will have a cup of tea, Fanny."

"Where have you been?" she asked, handing him his drink.

"I walked around the woods."

"Doing what?"

"Noticing things. As the owner, I should keep an eye on the property."

Cecil's eyes widened. "I am pleased to hear it, your grace. There is much to be done."

He had not thought of his cousin's response to his remark, and he cringed inwardly. "What have you been doing, Fanny?" he asked, in an effort to ward off the impending onslaught.

Cecil was not to be denied. "I do not have my notes with me, your grace, but there are several things I must discuss with you immediately." He launched into a list of needs, mentioning the chimney repair to one of his tenants' cottages, the fencing repairs required around one of the estate's pastures, and the progress regarding the payment negotiations with the stable carpenter.

John sat, sipping his tea and nibbling on the food, impressed and appalled. If his cousin could recite all these needs without his notes, John shuddered at what he faced when presented with an official report.

"In addition," Cecil said, "there is a cowshed that Farmer Puckworth needs built. His herd has expanded, and he needs more protection for them."

"An admirable worker," John said and focused his attention on his ward. "Fanny, you have not told us of your day."

Cecil did not notice the conversational turn. "Yes, Farmer Puckworth's mind is more open than those of most of your tenants. I admire his attempts to do things the modern way. I anticipate his cowshed—"

"Cecil," John interrupted. "Is a cowshed the proper topic over tea with a lady present?"

Halted in midrush, his cousin's mouth flapped like a fish for a second before Cecil regained his composure and said, "What lady?"

Fanny glared. "Me."

She didn't call him rude, but the insult hung in the air, unsaid. Cecil glared back, but he subsided at the admonition.

John did not want any bickering. He had enough to handle because of his deception. "Fanny, tell us about your day."

She straightened her posture, and a smile flitted across her face at being the center of attention. "My friend Lydia Grenville called today."

John's pulse quickened at the mention of her name. "She did?"

"You haven't met her yet, but she is my closest friend," Fanny said. "We had planned to have our London Seasons together until your brother's passing prevented it."

"You will go this spring," John promised.

"Lydia will probably go again, too. She returned without becoming betrothed." Fanny nodded with significance. "Something must have gone terribly wrong if she did not receive any offers."

"How do you know she didn't?" John challenged, annoyed at the girl's insinuation. "Perhaps they were not acceptable."

"If one had been acceptable, she would have snatched it," Fanny said. "You don't know what Lydia is like."

After Lydia's description of her Season, John thought he did know her. "I am certain she is not as you paint her."

"No?" Fanny sipped her tea before imparting her assessment. "Lydia is a woman on the prowl for the best marriage she can wheedle out of an unsuspecting aristocrat."

"Fanny! That is a harsh thing to say about a girl you call a friend."

A smug smile appeared on her face. "Harsh or not, it's the truth."

"I refuse to believe she is as predatory as you imply."

"I think I know her better than you do," Fanny said. "But

you will have a chance to meet her. We've been invited to dine at the manor the evening after the next. You'll meet her, and you'll see just how right I am."

Dine at Grenville Manor! John stared at her in shock. Yes, he would see, and he did not look forward to it.

Chapter Four

*T*he butler Newton met Lydia at the front door. "Good afternoon, miss."

The tone of his voice caused her to pause, yet she could read nothing in his impassive expression. "Is something wrong?"

"We have callers for tea, miss."

Apprehension and relief warred within her. Relief won. Her mother would never scold her in front of callers. "Who is here?"

He took the pencils and sketchbook she handed him. "Mrs. Fisher and her daughter."

Lydia's hands stilled in untying her bonnet, and some of her relief dimmed. "Oh, dear."

He said nothing in reply, but she thought she read sympathy in his eyes. She gave him the bonnet and pasted a charming smile on her face. "I shall go and welcome them."

In the drawing room, the afternoon sunlight poured through the tall Palladian windows, casting a summer's glow to the yellow and green room. The brightness did not lift Lydia's spirits when she entered. "Good afternoon, Mrs. Fisher and Mary." She kissed her mother's cheek. Only the stiffness of her mother's spine revealed how upset she was. "I am sorry to be late, Mother."

Lydia accepted the tea her mother poured and sat on the chair next to Mary. Dressed in pink, the girl possessed carefully arranged light brown hair and a properly pale complexion. Now twenty years of age, Mary had had a Season a couple of years ago, but her notorious shyness did not transplant well to the frantic bustle of the London social scene. She returned home before the Season was half finished and hid in the protective remoteness of the countryside. Lydia had a greater empathy for Mary's unbetrothed state. It would not be easy conversing with her, but Lydia preferred to delay her mother's reproaches as long as possible.

"How have you been?" Lydia asked.

Mary dropped her gaze and mumbled. "Fine, thank you."

"It is a beautiful summer day for a drive. Have you called on our neighbors?"

"No. Just you." Mary made no effort to continue the conversation with a question of her own. Her eyes remained lowered, and her hands were clasped in her lap.

Lydia repressed a sigh. She had known the social task of entertaining her guest would not be easy, but Mary made it more than difficult. She considered introducing the topic of her London Season and rejected the thought. Mary would only say "yes" or "no" at appropriate intervals, and Lydia did not currently feel capable of declaiming a monologue on the subject.

"Have you called on the new duke?" Lydia did not need to specify his name. There was only one in the neighborhood.

"Yes," Mary said.

Naturally. Mary might lack animation, but Mrs. Fisher had enough belligerence for a squad of soldiers. She would make it her mission to bring Mary to his notice.

"What kind of a man is he?" Lydia asked.

Forced to respond with something other than a yes or no answer, Mary paused to think. Then she shuddered. "Quite frightening, actually."

"Frightening? How?"

Mary's eyes widened into round circles. "I should not have said that."

Lydia was not about to allow Mary to retreat, not when the girl had just uttered the most interesting statement in her limited repertoire of conversation. Lydia leaned forward, inviting confidences. "Come, Mary. Tell me more."

"I meant to say he is a very kind man."

"You must elaborate. Why is he frightening?"

"I made a mistake. He is the duke, after all, and is above our petty opinions."

This vein of conversation grew more and more interesting. "What did he do?"

"He did not do anything. He barely spoke. He just looked at me while he drank his tea." Mary's voice held the desperation of one cornered.

"He only looked at you?" Lydia echoed. She studied Mary more closely, but the girl remained only passably pretty and without any animation. Mrs. Fisher supplied the warrior spirit.

"As if I were a bug." Mary's blue eyes glistened. "It was awful."

Lydia hastened to reassure her. "Maybe he is shy."

"A girl may be shy," Mary said, "but not a duke. He should talk to me or ignore me. Not stare at me."

Considering, Lydia sipped her tea. There was something to what Mary said. A man raised to the position of a duke would not be shy. He could not be. Arrogance would be his natural condition. Only the king or a prince possessed more power than a duke—Winterbourne must know that his every word, his every gesture, or as in Mary's circumstance, his every look—would be noticed and thoroughly discussed as those surrounding him searched for hidden meanings. No one wanted to offend a duke. Prudent people discovered his wishes and did them.

Lydia abandoned her disbelief that his look had frightened Mary. Plainly, something about the duke had stirred a deep response. Mary had never spoken so freely about anything or anyone before.

"Why did he stare?" Lydia asked.

Mary's lower lip trembled. "I never know what to say. You know how hard it is for me to talk—especially with a gentleman. Should not a proper girl be quiet and modest?"

Lydia heard echoes of society's dictates in Mary's words, but she doubted Mrs. Fisher had ever meant her daughter to take them so much to heart. For herself, Lydia had always found that a flirtatious aura did wonders in attracting men to her side, but she was certainly not going to point that out. Now she should concentrate on learning about Winterbourne.

"But for him to not converse during a call . . ." Lydia let her words trail off to invite further disclosures.

Mary obliged. "Strictly speaking, we did not call upon him, but upon Fanny. He was already in the drawing room, taking tea, when we arrived."

So he was not as rude as Mary had initially portrayed. "Yes?" Lydia encouraged.

"Mother timed our call in hopes he would be there, as all of our previous calls had failed to meet him. He stood and bowed when we were introduced. I did as Mother had commanded and sat near him."

"And then?"

"And then he stared. Should he not have conversed with me?"

"He said nothing to you? Nothing at all?"

"He complimented me on my dress, as a gentleman should. I was wearing my pink striped dress that Mother says I look quite well in. I said thank you. After a pause, he asked about our calls, and I said the castle was our only stop that day. Another moment passed before he asked if I had read anything of interest recently. I told him no. You know a young lady should only read improving works, and those are dull under the best of circumstances." Mary sighed. "After that, he said nothing more. He just drank his tea. It was so frightening to sit under his gaze."

Lydia bit her tongue. She should offer platitudes of reassurance, but she could not find the necessary words. From Mary's description, Lydia felt a deep sympathy for Winterbourne. He had manfully tried to chat with the girl, only to have every attempt sink into the bottomless well of Mary's shyness. Still, it intrigued her that one of his polite attempts had asked about her literary tastes—and that Mary had responded so strongly to his presence.

"Is he a handsome man?" she asked.

"Of course. He is a duke."

"I meant is he dark or fair?"

It seemed an obvious observation, yet Mary pondered for a moment. "I do not know."

Lydia blinked in astonishment. "Did you not see him?" After all, according to Mary, he had stared quite openly.

"I just remember how frightening he was." Mary shuddered.

It was Lydia's turn to stare as she realized Mary had seen nothing except her own emotions. She had envisioned herself the heroine of an Encounter, noticing nothing outside of herself. Mary had expressed herself so freely to Lydia because she had talked about herself—and only about herself.

Mrs. Fisher stood, signaling that their call was at an end. The usual flurry of farewells commenced until only Lydia and her mother were left in the room.

Lydia plunged in before her mother could speak. "Do you know what Mary told me? They called upon Winterbourne, and he frightened Mary with his look. I know she can be a ninny, but do you think—"

"Lydia." Her mother's voice cut across her defensive prattle with the sharp stroke of a master cook.

Dropping her gaze to the floor, Lydia knew she would not escape the reproachful lecture. "Yes, Mother."

"Where were you?"

"Out sketching." Her mother's sigh squeezed her heart with repentance. "I am sorry. I lost track of the time."

"It seems you are doing that more and more lately."

"I will try to do better."

Her mother approached and slid an arm across Lydia's shoulders. "So you have said previously, yet your lateness has not changed." She turned Lydia toward her.

Her mother's face was not angry. Lydia could have borne that easier than the disappointment she saw there. "I am truly sorry," she repeated with sincerity.

Her mother's sigh caused Lydia's regret to swell. "You cannot be always slipping off to sketch. I know you enjoy it, but it is only a diversion. You are a young lady now. A debutante. You must be available for these calls," her mother said.

"It was only Mrs. Fisher and Mary," Lydia offered in feeble defense.

"Even so, if you had loitered any longer you would have missed an opportunity. Mary has called upon the duke. She was able to tell you about him."

"She told me nothing terribly important, unless you think his inability to converse with Mary is news. I certainly learned he needs someone to help him keep a conversation going."

"And, my dear, that plays to your strength. You are quite capable of charming any man when you set your mind to the task. The duke will be smitten by you."

"I need to meet him first," Lydia muttered, wishing artifice was not required for her marriage.

"He will be coming to dinner the night after tomorrow. I pray you will not be late for that." Her mother's tone allowed for no disobedience.

Lydia had no intention of failing her duty. "I will be there, Mother, and I will be charming."

A smile flitted across her mother's face. "I know you will. Winterbourne cannot help but be enchanted. It will be a brilliant match."

Her mother hugged Lydia, and the girl clung to her, seeking the security that her parents' love had always provided.

"Mother," she asked, "what if I do not make a brilliant match? What if I fail to attract the duke?"

"Nonsense. You are beautiful, accomplished, and well dowered. You will capture his notice."

"But if I don't?" Lydia pulled away, uncertain.

"If you do not get the duke, we will still love you. After all, you are our daughter." Laughter hinted in her mother's voice at the thought of this absurd possibility.

"But what if I am wed to someone who is not titled?" She wanted to say aloud, *Someone like Alexander Penhope,* but she did not dare.

"Not titled? Put such foolishness from your mind. Your father would never accept an offer for your hand from someone who is not noble—and quite rightly, too."

"A man can be noble and not be titled."

Her mother hugged her close again. "My silly, sweet child, we want only the best for our girl. You are the treasure of our hearts. All you must do is be your attractive self, and all shall be well."

"Mother, why must I marry well? After all, I have you and Papa. I want a marriage like you have."

"I want the same for you, too. Come." She led Lydia over to the couch, where they sat down together, her mother's arm still around her. "Do you think your father will accept just any titled man?"

"No," Lydia said slowly. "I know he refused those two last summer when I asked him to do so."

"Then why do you doubt him now?"

"Because we are back home, and I am not betrothed. I had a whole Season in which to become engaged, and I did not."

"And you think we are desperate?"

Lydia fiddled with her skirt, pleating and unpleating it between her fingers. "There is the duke and the push to gain his notice."

"Yes, and he would make an admirable husband for you."

"How can you say that when we have never even met?"

"Do you think your father and I have not been listening to reports about this man's habits? He appears to be quiet and studious, with no disgusting habits reported by the gossip. Sensible people should find that a solid basis for affection to grow." Her mother gathered Lydia's hands into her own. "We love you, daughter. Do not fear that we will wed you where fondness cannot be nurtured. A good man will provide you with security for the future."

"Can the future be secured?" Lydia asked with some sadness.

"You are old enough to know nothing is promised in this

world, but wealth and a title can grant as much safety as possible."

"They did not protect the French aristocrats during the Terror."

Her mother's grip tightened. "Are you so determined to be obstinate? Your father and I are trying to safeguard you the best we can. You must be married. A woman alone is the prey of all sorts of terrible things. We will not be able to protect you forever."

"But must it be now?" Lydia beseeched. "Nothing is going to happen to you. Not now."

"No one can foretell the future. Opportunity must be seized when it appears. I don't want to lose my little girl, and if you marry the duke, you will not be so very far away." Her mother looked her straight in the eyes. "It would be a good match. Make an effort, Lydia."

Against her mother's love and concern, Lydia said, "I will do my best."

"Good girl." After a final approving squeeze of her hands, her mother released her and stood. "We must dress for dinner now. It is just us tonight, so that cook can devote her energies to our meal with the duke."

The next morning the enchantment of the woods could not quell Lydia's discontent at her mother's matrimonial scheming. One part of her hoped Alexander would escape to their clearing, while the other part recognized he must perform his secretarial duties.

She spread her blanket on the ground, propped her sketchbook on her knees, and with a pencil brought forth the subject dominating her mind. The picture of Alexander. She was alone, yet not lonely, here in the sanctuary the two of them had created.

A slight breeze ruffled the hem of her skirt. Birds hidden by the leaves chirped their songs. Although the leaves were still green, a few had golden-tipped edges, warning of the autumn to come. She was caught up in the care necessary to draw, but she was also resolved to watch the time. She would not be late for the duke's dinner.

Her portrait of Alexander was developing well. Using charcoal, she skillfully defined the planes of his face with different stroke thicknesses and smudges. She had his straight nose, the dishevelment of his hair after the climb through the forest, and the set of his ears. What surprised her most about the image was that somehow she had caught his quiet air of studiousness. The look in his eyes was friendly, accepting, and it snagged her heart.

Lydia never had any trouble talking with Alexander. Unlike Mary, he did not need the conversation centered upon him in order to participate. He had accepted without question Lydia's whimsical talk—even when she called herself a fairy princess. To be free from society's rigid expectations was intoxicating. As much as she wanted their friendship to continue, she knew their secret meetings in the woods would jeopardize any chance she might have to marry the duke. Her pencil stilled, and she stared at her sketchbook in dismay. It was even dangerous for her to possess this picture of Alexander.

Yet when she heard the shuffle of leaves announce someone's approach, she greeted Alexander with a smile. "Once again there is an intruder in the land of the fairy princess."

He bowed in response. "He begs permission of the fair lady to trespass in this clearing—which does *not* belong to her."

She giggled, swept by the feeling of acceptance his presence always produced. "Sit down and tell me what you have been doing."

He sat on the edge of the blanket she had left free for him. A thrill skipped through her at his nearness.

"I am far more interested in what you are doing. What are you drawing?" he asked.

She suddenly remembered her subject and flipped the cover of the sketchbook over her drawing. "You would not be interested."

"On the contrary. I am always interested in what you draw. You have such skill."

Heat burned up her neck and infused her face. "You flatter me."

He held out his hand. "Let me see it."

"No." Lydia clutched the book close to her chest.

"Very well, then." His hand dropped, and he lay back to rest upon one elbow. "Whom have you been calling upon?"

She did not answer immediately. "Aren't you going to tease me to show it you?"

"No." His gaze was clear and direct. There was no guile in those hazel eyes. "You have the right to keep your art hidden until you are ready to show it."

He was different from any man she had ever known—and her whole purpose in life was to meet as many eligible ones as possible. All of them would have teased and begged to get their way. Not Alexander. He accepted her decision. He respected her wishes. Lydia's hold on the book loosened.

"Mrs. Fisher and her daughter, Mary, called on us yesterday."

"Who are they?" His brow wrinkled. He looked so endearing that Lydia committed his expression to memory so she might sketch it later.

"She is a shy girl. She told me about her call upon the duke. He frightened her."

He sat up in astonishment. "Frightened her? How?"

"He looked at her," Lydia gravely informed him.

"He looked at her?" Alexander stared.

"Yes. Just as you are doing now."

His gaze pulled away. "I am sorry. Did I frighten you?"

She laughed and stretched out a hand to reassure him. "Of course not. Mary is a goose. She could not even tell me if the duke is dark or fair, so focused was she upon her fear."

"I am sorry she was frightened."

"It is not your fault."

His shoulders straightened. "Lydia, there is something I must tell you. It has been too long already."

Distress at his serious tone dampened her light spirits. "What is wrong?"

"You know I am not Alexander."

"Yes, I know. We've discussed that." She shifted forward in her concern. The sketchbook fell from her grasp and landed between them, the cover open. Her portrait of him gazed up at them.

"What's this?" he asked.

She snatched it up, but it was too late. He had seen her picture.

"That was a picture of me, wasn't it?"

"Please. I never meant to show it to you."

"May I see it now?"

Why should she try to hide it now? The secret was the fact that she had sketched him, not the drawing itself. Slowly she extended it to him. He took it gently in his hands and studied it while she held her breath.

"You drew a very flattering portrait of me," he said. "I am

honored. I don't remember sitting for you. Did you do this from memory?"

There was no sense in denying it. She had spent so much time thinking of him that his features, the very essence of his character, were imprinted on her mind. "Yes."

He studied the picture a moment longer. "My compliments on your skill are inadequate. You draw not only the outer mask but capture the inner soul, too."

"I sketch what I see."

"Then you are very perceptive." He held the sketchbook out to her.

She took it and looked at it, still seeing only her portrait. "What do you mean?"

"Can you not see the deeper meaning of what you have drawn?"

The hair, the eyes, the mouth, all of his features were as she had remembered them. Now that he stood before her, she saw where she had been amiss. The shape of the ear was not exactly correct, and she should probably alter the angle of his nose just a bit, yet it was plainly Alexander's face on the paper. She had caught his character, but she did not see the inner soul he referred to. She shook her head.

"When I look at that picture," he said, "I see a lonely man."

"Lonely?" She examined it more closely and saw what he meant. She had drawn his features accurately, but somehow her pencil strokes had drawn forth more—a solitary man, one who lived apart. She looked at him. "I did not realize what I sketched. I meant no offense."

"I am not offended. It is the truth."

The truth. What an odd thing to declare. She gazed at him in wonder. His eyes met hers without wavering. The hazel was so clear she knew there was no artifice, no flirtation in his words. Truth was what he spoke.

"Are you lonely?" she asked, making her voice low and gentle.

He turned away then. The bond between them seemed to break. Leaning forward, she placed her hand on his arm. "I am sorry."

He looked down at where she touched him. "Are you sorry for me or for you?"

"For me?"

"Surely you could only draw with such perception, if you were lonely, too."

Affronted, she straightened. "I am not lonely. I've been to many parties . . . when I was in London. You would be amazed at how sociable I can be. Sometimes there were three in one night."

"You are not in London now." His face was very close to hers. She could see the plane of his cheek, the strength of his chin, and the lashes outlining his eyes. Tenderness filled them—and something more.

She paused before whispering, "No, I am not."

And then her breath caught.

Their faces were scant inches apart. The woods became exceedingly still. The birds hushed their songs. Even the buzz of the insects quieted. It was as if nature joined Lydia in holding her breath—waiting.

He bent forward. With the lightest of touches, his lips brushed over hers. His stroke was gentle and sweet, a true example of his nature. When he lifted his head, a fleeting regret flashed through her. Her taste of him had been too short. She curved her lips into an invitation.

This time when he leaned forward, her hands caressed his shoulders, even as his cupped her head. She felt the roughness of his coat beneath her fingers, but when his lips met hers again, she forgot all about fabric, the woods, everything. Her world centered on him.

The kiss deepened. Her lips parted and met his mouth fully and completely. A slow exploration ensued through the softness. One where touch dominated.

No kiss she'd ever had before had caused this pounding of her heart or this humming of her blood. She wanted him. Desire developed within her like an artist beginning a picture, captured by the throes of creation. One stroke added to another until the masterpiece erupted onto the paper—complete.

Except she could not be completed by a ducal secretary.

Her eyes widened, and she pushed him away, one hand pressed to her mouth. His breathlessness matched her own.

"We should not have done that," she said, torn between regret and guilt.

He caught his breath and began, "It is my fault—"

"No." She started to reach out a hand to reassure him but then thought better of touching him. Her hand dropped to her lap. "I was a willing partner."

"But a gentleman—"

"No." Her refusal was louder this time. "We shall keep this quiet. No one must know about it." She glanced around the woods. This clearing had become a refuge. The trees acted as a protective veil. "It will be our secret."

He cleared his throat. "Lydia, there is something you must know."

She scrambled to her feet. "No! Don't speak another word. It can never happen again." In a flurry, she gathered up her materials and sketchbook, dropping two pencils in the process. She grabbed them and clutched them tightly to her heart.

She looked down at him, seeing the concern etched on his face. His hair was rumpled, probably from their kiss. He appeared so endearing, yet she should never, could never, allow any feelings to exist between herself and a ducal secretary. She could not fail so at her duty.

In a voice as steady as she could make it, she said, "I will see you at dinner at our house. We will meet as strangers. We must."

He stood up. "Lydia, you must listen to me."

"I must not! I dare not!" She whirled and ran away, leaving him standing on the blanket.

She tore through the woods, dodging the bushes and roots waiting to snag the unwary. Tears filled her eyes, and she bit her lip, hoping the physical pain would distract her from the pain in her heart.

She had played with passion. A moan of distress escaped her lips. For the first time, she had wanted a man. All those previous attempts at kissing while in London had been nothing but actions to be coldly analyzed. None of them had mattered.

Alexander stirred her. He brought her to the boiling point. Now she knew why she had been warned against allowing liberties. It wasn't because of the ruinous effect on her reputation. It wasn't because an innocent girl should not compare the kissing techniques of her suitors. It was because of what she might experience with a most unsuitable man. This overpowering passion could consume a girl, causing her to forget the duties she owed. For the rest of her life she would have to live with the memory, knowing no one else could ever repeat the feelings within her. She was destined for the duke, not his cousin.

That was the worst realization of all.

Chapter Five

*W*hen Lydia dashed away, John took two steps to follow before he halted. He could not forget the rejection implied when she had pulled back from his touch. The kiss, which had overwhelmed him in a storm of passion, had caused her to shrink from him, to refuse another caress from him. Pain pierced him with the sharpness of a Spartan spear.

Why was he surprised? Never had he done anything right with a woman, and never had he met one as bright and beautiful and friendly as Lydia. She resembled one of those Greek wood nymphs the gods encountered with such regularity in the ancient forests. She was his Lydia-of-the-woods.

She had spun her enchantment well. She had peeked into his soul with her sketch, and unexpectedly he had realized she could view him so clearly only if she was lonely, too. A bond of empathy arced between them. Common sense and logic fled before the power of his emotions. Her floral perfume scented the air around him, drawing him closer, urging him on. When he had turned his head and found her lips only inches from his, a wild daring had engulfed him. Her lips were soft beneath his, and he had willingly tasted and touched.

She did not shrink from him then. No, not then. It was his

crude handling of their kiss afterward that had frightened his Lydia-of-the-woods into vanishing. He did not know the poetic words to utter in such situations. He had tried to apologize for his actions, but without a guide to navigate the storm of passion tossing his reason awry he had uttered the wrong words. He had splintered the enchantment to shards, and with its destruction, his wood nymph had also disappeared.

He sighed and bent to pick up the blanket she had forgotten, folding it so the corners met precisely. He intended to return it to her the next time they met.

His hands slowed, then halted. Their next meeting was at dinner—where she would meet the Duke of Winterbourne.

Nausea rocked his stomach—a warm and choppy mass that felt like the curds formed from whey. For one wild moment, he thought of sending a note canceling the engagement for dinner due to illness. He certainly felt awful enough for the excuse to be true.

His absence would not protect him from the exposure of his deception, though. Cecil was also included in the invitation, and he would attend. When Lydia met him, she would wonder who "Alexander" truly was. Lydia was intelligent. It would not take her more than a moment to connect her fairytale partner with the missing duke.

Sending a note of regret would only add to the pile of shame his cowardice had created.

Alexander the Great was not a coward. He carried the battle to his enemies. Just witness the results when he demanded the surrender of Sogdiana Rock. From the top of their high fortress, the defenders had jeered, "Find soldiers with wings." That night, Alexander's soldiers scaled the Rock with ropes. Alexander conquered the Rock, but it was also written that when he saw Roxana, the daughter of a nobleman, he fell in love with her and married her. Boldness bore Alexander to his destiny.

Perhaps boldness could also save his fake namesake in the year 1804. John hoped so, but he doubted it. He squared his shoulders. He would meet his fate.

Carrying the blanket, he trudged back to the castle. It sprawled below him as he skidded down the ridge, his steps reckless. The nearer he came, the larger it grew until it filled his vision, a reminder of who he was. The burden of his identity weighed heavier and heavier. John straightened his spine until he reached his full height. What cannot be avoided must be endured.

As he traversed the stone steps, Scott, his well-trained butler, opened the front door. "Good afternoon, your grace."

The man obviously kept close watch on his master's comings and goings—and he never asked about where the duke went. Suddenly John was grateful for that reticence.

He returned the greeting, and because he should, he asked, "Has anyone called?"

"No, your grace."

Fanny entered the hall. "You're back!"

"Good morning, Fanny," John said.

"It will not be morning for much longer. You're just in time for luncheon." She strolled over to him. "Where have you been?"

"Out walking," he replied and hoped she would leave it at that.

"You are doing quite a bit of walking lately."

"It does a man good to stride over his property."

She made a moue of distaste. "You sound like Cecil."

John knew that was not a compliment.

"Don't be like him, always prosing on about the estate. It would be far more exciting if you had a secret rendezvous."

Involuntarily, his fingers clutched the blanket. "Why would it be exciting to do something so improper?"

Fanny sighed. "Because then something would be happening around here. Nothing ever happens."

"You have a good life. You are fed and well clothed." He eyed her rose gown with its lace and embroidery.

"As if that is all my life should be. Animals in the farmyard are fed and cared for. I want more. I'm still waiting for my Season. I do nothing but wait. It's dull, dull, dull! Secrets are exciting."

"Secrets can also mean behavior to be ashamed of."

"Only if one is caught. Besides, scandal is exciting."

"Fanny! That is a terrible thing to say!"

"Oh, pooh! I don't mean for me. Watching someone else's, now that would be something to see."

"Such sentiments make you sound cruel."

She stamped her foot. "You don't understand."

He didn't understand her, but he did understand behavior that had to be kept hidden. "Spring will be here eventually, and then you will go to London and have a smashingly successful Season."

She rolled her eyes. "What are you carrying?" she asked, stepping closer to see.

"This?" He lifted the blanket as if realizing for the first time what he held. His heartbeat quickened. "It's just an old blanket."

"It looks like it came from the stables."

"It probably did," he agreed.

She sniffed, but he knew it did not carry the odor of horses.

"Why do you have it?" she asked.

"I must have picked it up."

John handed it to the butler. "See that this is taken up to my room."

"Yes, your grace." The butler bowed and left to hand the task off to a footman.

"Your room?" Fanny asked. "Should it not go back to the stables?"

"I didn't find it there."

"Where?"

"During my walk."

"Was it someplace secret?" Her nose practically twitched, as if she picked up a lingering scent.

"No." He made his voice firm. "Fanny, your desire for excitement is leading you into fantasy."

He had lingered long enough. To forestall any further probing, he hurriedly said, "You said luncheon was served. I will wash up and join you directly." He strode up the stairs toward his room.

Fanny called after him, "You don't need to rush. The servants will wait for *you*."

It was a reminder that because of his rank, his wishes came first. Fanny felt trapped by society, but he was just as much a prisoner of the same expectations. A cage, no matter how gilded, is still a cage.

He tried to shake off the oppressive reminder as he walked down the paneled hall past the painting displaying a chase between horse and fox across the countryside. Had the fox escaped the hunt? Fanny possessed the tenacity of a hunting hound. John had narrowly escaped revealing his meetings with Lydia. They were a secret and, according to his logic, thus shameful. He knew to whom the shame belonged, and it was not Lydia. That blanket had been a noticeable clue, and to have sent it to his rooms . . .

John shook his head at his carelessness. For him to overlook such a detail meant the kiss had truly addled his brain. He could only hope he had managed to blunt Fanny's suspicions.

By the evening of the dinner, Fanny and her concerns no longer devoured John's thoughts. The upcoming dinner at Grenville Manor consumed all of his attention. As he dressed with his valet's assistance, John's gaze kept straying toward the blanket. It lay folded on top of the trunk at the foot of his bed, a symbol of an enchantment soon to be broken by reality.

His valet, Howard, did excellent work in keeping the room neat and John's clothes presentable. However, John had to admit that his own rebellion regarding the changes to his station in life did not give his man much to work with. It came as a shock to see that the well-used blanket did not look out of place among the rest of the surroundings. Old coats and comfortable mended shirts did not turn out a duke in the first stare of fashion.

Tonight, however, John had armored himself as the Duke of Winterbourne. His coat of black superfine had been tailored to show the breadth of his shoulders and the trimness of his waist. His white linen gleamed, and the golden embroidery festooning his waistcoat glimmered when the light touched it. Starch held the creases of his cravat with a precision any dandy would have approved. The emerald pin with gold filigree nestled among the folds in the most tasteful fashion.

John nodded with approval at the image in the looking glass. "A good job, Howard."

His man stepped back and made a final inspection. Pleasure beamed on his face. "Thank you, your grace."

John looked again at his reflection. The man in the looking glass appeared to be a stranger, but not enough of one to hide the truth. Not to Lydia. Not to her discerning artist's eye. She would recognize him. Clothes may make the man, yet she had already looked beneath the outer trappings and seen the loneliness in his soul.

He had always considered himself an honest man. A scholar who studied the facts. How had he allowed the deception to grow and grow until it possessed as many heads as the Hydra? Because he was a coward when dealing with women. Because he wanted Lydia to think well of him. He sighed and lifted his chin. There was no avoiding the moment of discovery.

John had seen Grenville Manor from the edge of the woods, and now his carriage rolled right up to the front steps, giving him a closer view. The white building was much smaller than Winterbourne Castle. The manor's size did not overwhelm him the way his own castle did. Although it was barely dusk, candles lit the windows in a welcoming fashion. John climbed the steps to the front door, his legs shaking. Amazingly, his wobbling steps did not cause him to stumble. Neither his fellow passengers, Fanny and Cecil, nor any of the servants seemed to notice that anything was wrong with him.

They could not hear the pounding of his heart, either, but John could. Loud and sonorous. Each thump reverberated in his ears, almost blocking out the polite expressions of welcome from the Grenville butler, who led them across the entry hall to the drawing room where the family—and his fate—awaited.

"The Duke of Winterbourne," the butler proclaimed.

John paid no attention to the rest of the formal announcement of their arrival. His gaze sought out, and instantly found, Lydia. She stood next to her parents, a sweet maiden dressed in blue, her blond hair up, with curls cascading from the ribbon entwined around her head. It matched the one tied under her breasts. Her lips were full and red. He had kissed them. Could he expect mercy from her mouth when he did not deserve it? Her lips curved into a friendly smile. He watched as the smile turned into a circle of disbelief and her eyes widened with shock. He knew her surprise was not a happy one. His muscles stiffened as his doom enveloped him.

The etiquette of greetings carried John through the next moments until Josiah Grenville presented her. "My daughter, Lydia."

She curtseyed very low, as deeply as she would to a king. "Your grace, welcome to our home."

Not by a look or a gesture did she hint at their previous meetings. He bowed in response, telling himself he was relieved that shock had not caused her to reveal their secret. "Miss Grenville."

She rose and looked him directly in the eyes. "Your grace, I am honored to meet you at last."

Was it his conscience pricking him or did she emphasize *you*? "It is I who am honored."

He knew the correct response to an introduction. Her face appeared perfectly welcoming, but in her eyes hurt and anger tumbled. He had caused those feelings. It was his fault they existed in her. Shame washed over him with its condemning warmth.

"Dinner will be ready soon," came the voice of her mother.

Her father gestured toward an upholstered wing chair. "Perhaps your grace would like to sit here?"

He sat. As the daughter of the house, Lydia gracefully seated herself on the couch beside her father and unfurled her fan. Poised and elegant, she posed as if she sat for her portrait. Her blue dress deepened the blue in her eyes, which now peered at him from over the edge of her fan. Although her beauty easily overwhelmed him, it had always been her eyes that put him at ease. Now there was nothing in them that induced comfort.

She fluttered her fan. "I understand your grace is interested in ancient Greece?"

Was she going to reveal their meetings after all? "Who told you that?" he demanded.

"Fanny and I often exchange calls, your grace. I must admit we have talked of you."

Fanny's lips stretched into a tight grimace supposed to be a smile. "Lydia broached the subject," she said in a warning tone meant to remind him of what she had told him about Lydia's marriage-minded ways. "She wanted to know everything about you."

With a light trill, Lydia broke in. "A handsome duke is always a topic for conversation." And she fluttered her eyelashes at him.

The gesture sliced him like a scythe through the fresh grass of summer. This girl was not his Lydia-of-the-woods. She looked like her, and she sounded like her, but this was another creature entirely.

"What do you know about Greece?" he asked.

"I know Alexander was a great soldier. So very *noble*. A man to be emulated."

He refused to be drawn into a discussion of his hero. John knew his actions did not measure up to any noble standards. Clearing his throat, he said, "Alexander was indeed a great warrior. His conquests spread Greek culture far and wide. Science, mathematics, and literature were carried along with his armies. Perhaps you have had a chance to read some of their stories?"

"No. I would enjoy hearing tell some of their tales. Do they have any about people in disguise?"

"The gods often disguised themselves when wooing maidens."

"So deception was a common form of courtship among the ancients?"

This conversation was treading in dangerous territory. Both her speech and the brittleness in her eyes warned him to beware. He glanced away and saw Cecil watching him with narrowed eyes, while a stiff smile was pasted on Fanny's face. There was no denying the proud beams emanating from the smiles of Lydia's parents. He swallowed. As much as he wanted to, he could not explain to Lydia. Not now. They were performing before an audience. He must not forget that.

He shifted the topic of conversation. "Greek plays cover many themes, deception included."

"Indeed, your grace?" Lydia leaned forward to display an air of interest. "Did any of them feature women?"

It was all playacting. "Sophocles wrote a drama titled *Antigone* that featured a woman as the main character."

"Was it about a nobleman deceiving a woman?"

She was not going to let go. He knew he had behaved badly, and he knew he must properly apologize, yet this was not the time or place.

Doggedly, he continued discussing *Antigone.* "No. It is a tale of courage and devotion. Antigone's brother took part in an uprising against the king, who successfully defeated the rebels. Her brother was one of those who died on the battlefield. As a lesson, the king decreed that the bodies should remain unburied. Antigone could not accept such a command."

"Why not?"

He saw she was interested. The fan no longer fluttered falsely between them. Hope began to stir within him. Perhaps not all was lost. "The Greeks believed if a body was left unburied, its soul was condemned to wander the earth, damned forever."

"In the same fashion, we bury a suicide at the crossroads."

"Yes, in unhallowed ground." Encouraged, he warmed to the telling of the tale. "Antigone could not allow her brother to be lost for eternity. First she asked the king's permission to bury her brother. He refused. In the end, she secretly went and did it anyway. When discovered, she paid for her disobedience with death."

"That's terrible! She was only trying to care for her brother."

"She disobeyed the king's commands. Those who break the laws must pay."

Lydia straightened, and her fan snapped shut. "She obeyed a higher law to protect her brother's soul."

"She should have obeyed her king." Fanny's voice cut in, reminding John that as much as he wished, he was not in that special clearing in the forest. He straightened on his chair.

Lydia's eyes flashed at Fanny's speech, but her voice remained pleasantly conversational. "It was courageous of her to obey her beliefs."

"Courageous?" Fanny said. "Foolish, I say. She knew the penalty, and she broke the law anyway."

"It was the king who was wrong."

"Lydia," her mother said. "Let the duke speak."

"Thank you," John said, pleased at how Antigone's story had gained Lydia's interest. "It is because of this very conflict, just now demonstrated by Fanny and Miss Grenville, that the play has resonated through the ages. To which does one owe the higher loyalty? The state or the gods? Each provides the rules that create a stable society and permit civilization to grow. The state is responsible for the temporal realm, while the gods protect the spiritual."

Ready to plunge more fully into the subject, he cast his glance around the room. His heart sank. Cecil sprawled in his chair, bored. Mr. and Mrs. Grenville were too polite to be so obvious, but their smiles appeared false and their interested gazes glued on. Fanny's narrowed eyes expressed her amusement at him.

He had been lecturing again.

As the duke, he commanded their attention. They would listen, but they would never truly participate. Such discussions did not animate them the way they did him. Silence followed the cessation of his speech.

"Since the gods are eternal and the state is not, certainly it is they who are greater," Lydia said, rescuing him from his embarrassment.

He turned to her in gratitude. The emotion stilled when she fluttered her fan at him like any debutante.

"I would agree with you," he said. "Your logic matches mine."

"It is not logic I believe in, your grace." Her smile was enchanting and her voice lilting. "But the power of one's heart."

She was flirting with him. He knew it and loathed the knowledge. Despite the prettiness with which her words were spoken, they rang false. The hollowness of their tone echoed through the emptiness within him. He knew why she spoke up for him. He was the Duke of Winterbourne, and she was Miss Grenville, who knew her duty to her station in life.

He felt more alone than ever. The forest enchantment was well and truly shattered.

*   *   *

He is the duke. The duke. The duke! Over and over that fact tolled through Lydia's mind with the soul-deep reverberation of the village church bell. Throughout dinner she managed to act like any debutante who knew her way around a place setting. She giggled and batted her eyelashes and fluttered her fan. Her surprise was great, but it could not last forever. It did wear off. Beneath her façade, a slow-burning anger began to glow in the embers of her shock.

When the men entered the drawing room to join the ladies after dinner, her gaze concentrated on him. Her father accompanied him and, as was usual when near an eligible suitor, praised her accomplishments. "My daughter excels at all the ladylike arts, your grace. You should hear her sing. She has a lovely, sweet voice, not an overdone one like those trained in the Italian tradition. She is very good at drawing, too."

Usually her father's boasting embarrassed Lydia, but not tonight. She wanted Winterbourne to know that she was not some bird-witted widgeon he could gull with impunity. He might be an educated scholar, but she possessed skills, too.

When her father led Winterbourne to the chair where she sat, Lydia asked, "Are you interested in sketching, your grace?"

"It is not an ability I possess, though I admire those who can draw."

His manner was tentative, and she was glad. He should feel mortified by his actions. She rose and covered the angry trembling of her fingers with a flirtatious waffle of her fan. "Some claim an artist can see into a subject's soul. Do you believe that might be the truth or just speculation?"

"I am not an artist, but perhaps there is some truth spoken there."

"I think it is speculation. I have known of an artist who was fooled by her subject."

"Lydia," came her mother's voice. The word was sweet and full of warning. *Do not disagree with the duke,* she implied.

Lydia wanted to do more than disagree. She wanted to rail at him. Tell him what she thought of his sly, deceitful actions. She couldn't. Not here. Not without revealing their secret meetings. He had met her falsely, but she had participated in deceit, too. She could not unmask him without revealing her part and destroying her social standing in scandal. He had trapped her. She would be the debutante that society—and he—expected her to be.

As though heeding her mother's silent warning, Lydia asked, "Are you a student of art, your grace?"

"Not of art specifically," Winterbourne said. "My interests lie more toward ancient Greece."

"Yes, that story you told of Antigone did spark my imagination. She should have buried her brother."

A small, hopeful smile tugged at the edges of his mouth. "I do agree with you. Antigone did the right thing."

"La, your grace!" She tapped him with her fan. "Does that mean you think emotions are stronger than intelligence? Why are you a scholar, then?"

"Intelligence should direct one's emotions. Otherwise, chaos prevails."

"That sounds more like Fanny's argument about rules than agreeing with me about the heart." Lydia giggled.

He glanced away, but not before she had seen the hurt in his eyes. She had scored in this strange confrontation between them. She could not express her anger outright, but she could use the mask of a debutante to say one thing while meaning another.

Behind Winterbourne, she saw her mother frown. Lydia bit her lip. Scoring points on the duke was not the way to attract his favorable notice. She knew how to truly capture his interest.

"Perhaps your grace would tell me another tale about the Greeks."

When he looked back at her, his face was wary. "I would not want to bore you."

"You did not bore me," she assured him. "Come tell me one about the gods. We can walk around the garden as you do."

She waited expectantly, and when he offered her his arm, she rose and took it. They strolled through the open French doors into the small walled garden where her mother's flowers flourished. The yellow and pink of dusk faded before the oncoming night. Already a half-moon hung in the purple-blue twilight. A soft breeze stirred, yet it did not chill Lydia's skin. Her blood was rushing too warm for the weather to cool it.

She broke the silence between them. "So tell me a tale of the gods. Are there any love stories?"

"Apollo was the god of love," he began and waited, as if uncertain he should continue.

"Yes?"

"He was also the sun god. He made the sun rise and set by riding across the sky from east to west in his blazing chariot."

"That is certainly a romantic image."

"But not scientific."

She peeked at him over her fan. "Does that matter?"

"Yes, it does." He halted and faced her. "Lydia, I behaved

badly toward you. I regret it, deeply, and I ask for your forgiveness."

She snapped her fan shut, dropping the flirtatious mask. "Why did you do it? Why allow me to think you were someone else?"

He looked at her a moment longer and then ran his hand through his hair, destroying the perfection of his appearance. His rumpled locks reminded her of how he had looked when they first met, like a secretary—or the student he truly was.

"I don't know if I can make you understand. I'm not sure I do myself." He squared his shoulders. "I never planned to deceive you. I only said Alexander was my name because I had been reading his biography. It was the first thing that popped into my head when I met you."

"But you let me think you were *Cecil* Penhope."

"I am not proud of that."

Although the pale moonlight lit his forehead and his cheeks, the approaching darkness shadowed his eyes, making it difficult for her to study them. He dressed in the sartorial elegance of a London nobleman, yet his disordered hair told her the splendid clothing was as much a façade as "Alexander." She wanted to rail at him and to understand him at the same time.

"What are you proud of?" she asked.

"Not much. I am ashamed of the way I treated you. That time in the woods was magical. The enchantment there was so powerful. I didn't have to be the duke."

He made no sense to her. She struggled to grasp what he was saying. "It was a masquerade? A game?"

"No, not a game. It was much too real for that. That is why I couldn't tell you the truth. I began badly and then lacked the courage to correct my deception. I never meant to hurt you."

He put his hands on her shoulders. In that instant, all the feelings and touch of his kiss sprang into full-blown remembrance. Her lips trembled.

"Can you forgive me?" he asked.

He was so close she felt the breath of his words as well as heard them. His hands lay warm on her shoulders, drawing her toward him. He was the duke, and he had deceived her. She should be angry with him. But she wasn't. She couldn't be. Not any longer. They were not in the woods, but its spell still lingered between them like the fine tendrils of ivy vines. The memory of their kiss still shook her to her soul.

"Of course, I forgive you." She tried to speak lightly, but her voice quavered in betrayal. To hide her feelings, she tapped him with her fan and said, "After all, a duke can do no wrong."

His jaw hardened. "And I am a duke."

"Of course, you are."

"Something you cannot forget."

"Forget? I just learned it."

He pulled away from her. "True. I must remember that." He offered her his arm. "Shall we continue our walk? The gardens are indeed beautiful."

She looked at his correctly positioned arm. It acted like a barrier between the two of them. Somehow, she had lost him. The bond between them did not exist outside the forest. She placed her hand upon it. "Of course. My mother is very proud of her flowers."

She would get him back. Her time in London had taught her how to attract a man. She wanted this one, and he would be hers. She could not, would not fail.

Chapter Six

*L*ydia spent a restless night, waiting for morning. Images of the duke at the dinner overlaid her memories of "Alexander," as he had appeared in the forest. The realization that they were one and the same man continued to stun her. She rolled onto her back and hugged the covers close, remembering his kiss.

Winterbourne's deception had angered her, but during the night she'd had time to reflect upon the situation. Despite his attempted explanation, she did not understand why he'd misled her, but she was not going to allow her incomprehension to block her path. She knew what she wanted.

Indeed, she was the most fortunate of girls. She had been richly blessed, for she could wed where both her duty and her desire ruled. She did not have to send away the man whose kisses stirred her blood. She could have him and the marriage that was her destiny. Her sigh was long and full of anticipation.

Now she had only to extract an offer from him. It should not be too difficult. Already a bond existed between them, forged in secrecy but also forged with affection.

Tomorrow it would all begin. She *would* see him again.

When morning came, she would go to their clearing in the woods.

She clutched a pillow tightly to her breast. Should she let him kiss her immediately or play the coquette at first? Both tactics had their merits. One method would let his passion lead them where it might. In the other, she would promise and entice for the wedding. Whichever one she adopted, there was no question about it; they would kiss again.

The duke was no more able to forget their kiss than she was. It had shimmered between them last night when they walked in the garden. Indeed, for a moment she had thought he might claim another one. Likely the nearness of her parents had prevented him from stealing it. A smile of expectation curved her lips. There were no parents in the forest.

On and off throughout the night she dozed. When dawn poked its rays into her bedroom, she was more than ready to greet it. She kicked at her sheets while waiting impatiently for her maid. Lydia wanted to dress and be on her way, yet it would not be wise to change her routine and arouse her parents' suspicions.

A slight knock heralded Meg's arrival. At last Lydia could rise and put on her wrapper over her chemise.

"What dress will you wear today?" Meg asked.

Lydia pondered. This was an important question. The blue sprigged one was her favorite, but she had been wearing the green one when Winterbourne kissed her. Or should she choose something he had not yet seen, such as the lilac-colored one? "Which one would you suggest?"

"Will you be calling at the castle, miss?" Meg asked.

"Yes, this afternoon." Lydia understood Meg's question. She was a competent ladies' maid. She understood the importance of a follow-up call after the first meeting with the duke last night.

"You'll want something that will impress him, then." She reached into the armoire and pulled out a pale yellow dress. "This looks well on you, miss."

Lydia hesitated. "The duke is a quiet man. He prefers his studies. You don't think it is too bright?"

Meg shook her head. "It's sunny and cheerful, miss. His grace will like the sunshine after his musty old books."

Lydia took the dress and held it in front of her before the looking glass. The color complemented her golden curls and bestowed a happy glow upon her complexion. Meg spoke truer than she knew. "Alexander" had been escaping. Maybe the prospect of sunshine in his life would appeal to him. After all, flowers enticed the bees with bright colors.

"Perhaps you are right," Lydia said. "I will wear the yellow, and I want my hair dressed in a simple style. Nothing too outrageous. I don't want him to shy off."

"Very good, miss."

Meg laid the dress on the bed, while Lydia sat before the looking glass. The maid picked up the brush and began to stroke Lydia's hair.

Lydia watched as Meg worked her skill. Perhaps it was because the maid was assisting in preparing the enticements for Winterbourne, but Lydia felt greatly in charity with her.

"Did you see the duke last night?" she asked Meg.

With the comb in her mouth, the maid shook her head.

"He is young," Lydia continued, "but I should have realized that. After all, George was the older half brother, and he was only five and twenty when he had his accident."

Meg used the comb to separate out a hank of hair. "Is his grace handsome?"

"He is a duke, so naturally one notices him. But if he wasn't . . ." Her voice trailed off as she considered Winterbourne's appearance. Before yesterday's discovery, did she think him handsome? With his light brown hair, hazel eyes, and lean figure, he could have been overlooked, but she had not.

"He has more than just his appearance to recommend him," Lydia said slowly. "There is a reticence about him. He almost seems vulnerable."

"Vulnerable to what, miss? He's a duke. Only the king or a prince is above him."

"That's true." Lydia gave a light laugh to cover her discomfort at speaking so truly. "It was a silly thought."

Meg stuck the last pin into Lydia's curls and stepped back to display the result. Lydia looked and was well pleased. The sides of her hair were pulled back over the ears to fall in a gentle tumble from a satin ribbon tied at her crown. It exuded simplicity. There was nothing about it to frighten off a retiring suitor.

Lydia nodded. "You've done well, Meg."

"Thank you, miss." She unrolled a pair of stockings and knelt to put them on Lydia.

She extended her foot and felt the cotton slide over her leg. She could see the top of Meg's head with her hair neatly arranged in a tight chignon. Her dress was a dark brown in a severe cut. Lydia suddenly remembered Meg mentioning a beau. How did the maid attract him dressed as she was?

"Did you see your man last night?" Lydia asked.

Startled, Meg glanced up. "Miss, I was waiting for you to come to bed."

Lydia knew better. "Nonsense. There were several hours between dressing me for dinner and bedtime. Come, you can tell me. Did you see him?"

Eagerness to chat warred with caution on Meg's face.

To encourage her, Lydia said, "You already told me he wants to buy an inn."

It was enough. Meg said, "I did see him last night."

"You didn't travel into town in the dark, did you? That's not safe."

"No, miss. We met at the end of the manor's drive."

"Well, I am glad of that," Lydia said. "My father is always telling me how dangerous the roads are."

"My Ben cares about me."

The pride in Meg's voice caused a pang of regret to shoot through Lydia. She could not rely on the care of her beloved. She could rely only on his rank. That must be sufficient for her. She was destined to be a duchess, and Meg could attract all the stableboys available while wearing dreadful-looking dresses. Immediately she regretted the unkind thought.

"Meg, would you like to have my pink dress?"

The maid plopped on the floor with astonishment. "Your pink dress, miss?"

The offer surprised Lydia, too. "You want to impress your Ben, don't you? The pink will look good on you." And she knew it only made herself appear washed out.

"Of course. Thank you, miss."

Pleasure glowed in Meg's face, making Lydia satisfied with her offer. Everything was going right in her world. Meg was content. Her parents would be pleased their daughter was about to become a duchess, and she was on her way to meet Winterbourne.

It had not been difficult to slip out of the manor after breakfast. As usual, her father raged at his newspaper, and her mother quizzed her about her plans to call at the castle that afternoon. Of course, Lydia would take tea with Fanny. She would even take tea with the true ducal secretary, so long as she met with Winterbourne.

So now she waited among the trees. She had her pencils and her sketchbook but had been unable to find her blanket.

It would be difficult to pretend she was drawing while standing up, but she doubted he would expect any masterpieces today. They had much to talk about.

At first she positioned herself leaning against a tree, but the rough bark soon caused her to itch. Then she stood in the center of the clearing where the branches formed a dappled pattern on her dress, but her legs grew stiff from standing still. So she began to stroll around the clearing in what she hoped was a romantic fashion. She paced the circle many times before she admitted it—he was not coming.

"It was only a setback. Just a minor one," Lydia assured herself as the carriage rolled toward Winterbourne Castle. "One cannot expect the passage to the rank of duchess to run smoothly."

Anything could have prevented his arrival in the woods this morning. After all, a duke had many demands upon his time. If he could not come to her, well, then, she would go to him. An afternoon call on Fanny to take tea provided the perfect excuse.

Bolstered by her sense of purpose, Lydia arrived at the castle and was shown into the small drawing room, where she greeted Fanny.

"I am so glad you called," Fanny said as she led Lydia to a seat on the couch.

Lydia smoothed her skirt into a nicely draped position. "After you were so kind as to come to dinner last night, I wanted to have a comfortable coze with you."

"You don't need to pretend with me. You want to discuss Winterbourne."

"I was very pleased to meet him," Lydia said, as any proper miss would.

"Pshaw!" Fanny leaned back and regarded her. "Now that

you've met him, what did you think? You see I was correct. He can only converse about ancient Greece. Every topic is directed that way."

"I found it interesting."

"Only because you are not required to hear about Socrates and Pericles at every turn."

"Who are they?"

Fanny wagged her finger. "Don't you start on me, Lydia. I know you too well. They are Greeks long dead and thus of no interest."

"That play he spoke about intrigued me."

"The *duke* intrigued you. You don't have to act the innocent miss with me. If you want to hear all about his Greeks, that is your affair, but he will not notice you as marriageable material. He knows nothing of women or society."

Lydia remembered their kiss, and a secret smile curled within her. Fanny was not as knowledgeable as she thought. Refusing to speak against the duke, Lydia said, "I found it rather refreshing to converse with someone about something other than repeating the gossip that everyone already knows."

"What gossip? Out here in the wilds of Essex nothing ever happens that can be talked about." Fanny crossed her arms petulantly. "This has to be the end of the world for excitement. At least you had a Season in London. A chance for society."

What, Lydia wondered, *am I, if not part of society?* To forestall any more of Fanny's complaints, she said, "Speaking of society, I was wondering if you will be ringing for tea?"

"You can have tea, if you want." Fanny picked up the silver bell sitting on the table beside her and shook it hard. The tinkling sound summoned the maid. Once the tea had been requested and the maid had departed, Fanny looked at Lydia. "It won't work, Lydia. Tea with me won't help you."

Lydia carefully made sure her slippers peeked out from under her skirt's hem. "You say the strangest things."

"You don't fool me. You hope having tea with me will bring Winterbourne into the room and under your influence." Fanny shook her head. "I pity you, if you succeed. You don't want lectures about the Greeks poured into your ears for the rest of your life, do you?"

"I am certain you exaggerate."

"No," Fanny said morosely, "I don't."

"Then, let's you and I discuss fashion." Lydia could not prevent the hint of exasperation in her voice. She didn't want to hear complaints about Winterbourne. They could sour the atmosphere before he came. Sweetness always lured better than vinegar. "Those who might enter for tea can join us in the conversation, too."

"You will see," Fanny warned, but she shrugged and capitulated. "Did you see the new dress that Mary Fisher wore to church last Sunday?"

"Was it new? I thought she might have only changed the trims."

John heard Lydia arrive. The lilt in her voice sang down the marble-floored hall and wafted through the open door of his library much like the melody with which the sirens enticed Ulysses. Her kiss haunted him. The passion, the emotion it fired within him stormed against the barricade of logic he had constructed. Against her wiles, his intellect had surrendered.

The kiss had been a surprise. If he had planned for it, the emotions would never have overwhelmed him. Indeed, he had done quite well last night at dinner. On guard for Lydia's attempts to charm a duke, he had been able to see right through her machinations. She had been revealed for the schemer Fanny had always declared she was.

He could face her again, secure in the knowledge that she did not have the power to disconcert him. He would not give it to her. He did not have to skulk here, hidden away in his book-lined refuge.

Except it was not a refuge.

Once again, he was trapped, listening to Cecil drone on and on. This time his cousin presented a report of which he was extremely proud. Based upon the quantity of statistics involved in calculating the crop yields—by field—for the last several years, Cecil had plainly done yeoman's work on his research.

When John complimented him on the effort, Cecil said, "It was not easy, your grace. The records kept under your brother's tenure before I arrived here are in a deplorable state. I must admit I cannot be certain that the yields tracked for our fields to the east of the Green Meadow are correct."

"You made your best effort. That is all anyone can expect."

"I think that tracking the yields of the various fields will give us a scientific basis for future decisions, showing where we need to fertilize or maybe even let a field lie fallow."

The glow on Cecil's face made John realize how seldom he paid attention to the work of running the dukedom. It all fell onto Cecil's shoulders. His cousin did good work, but John felt a splinter of guilt. It should be he who oversaw the planning. Cecil could do the detail work, but Alexander had run the empire.

John tried to concentrate on Cecil's numbers. They would have been easier to follow if he could have looked at them. Cecil preferred to read them out loud until the twos and threes jumbled with the percentages into a hodgepodge mess in John's mind.

The mental muddle did not protect him from remembering that he had avoided meeting Lydia in the woods that morning. Last night she had changed into the same kind of manipulative female as every woman he had met since assuming his rank. He could read the hopeful words *future duchess* on her forehead as if a typesetter had inked them. The knowledge announced itself within her eyes and in her facial expressions, and even her gestures with her fan seemed to spell out her plans. Listening to Cecil was his self-imposed punishment for his spinelessness in not facing Lydia.

However, he did not have to condemn himself to a task forever. Knowing she was just down the hall tempted him. Besides, last night had been a shock to her. Naturally his rank was at the forefront in her attitude toward him. He would be wrong to judge her too quickly. Meeting her again after the surprise had dissipated would be the rational approach.

It would also be a chance for him to evaluate her again, to prove that her appeal did not exist for him.

When he had to choose between Cecil and Lydia, she won. He pushed back his chair and stood.

"Your work is impressive," he said. "Surely your throat is getting parched from so much reading. Let us join Fanny for tea."

Cecil cleared his throat. "I don't mind if we continue working."

"But I do mind." John put his hand on Cecil's shoulder to urge him out of the room. "It is not right for you to work without ceasing."

"Truly, it is not an imposition. I like determining how our estates can be improved."

John did not permit Cecil's protests to sway him. Together

they went down the hall to the small drawing room. For only an instant before entering, John hesitated. Cecil looked at him, puzzled, and John went forward.

His gaze sought Lydia immediately. Dressed like a ray of sunshine, with a cunning hat perched rakishly on her golden curls, she greeted him with a welcoming smile. She was more beautiful than Helen of Troy could ever have been. His heart bounded upward in anticipation. Did he dare hope the shock of discovery had worn off? Was she still his Lydia-of-the-woods, even if they met for tea in the castle?

He strode forward and took the chair next to her. "Miss Grenville, it is good to see you again."

"I *so* enjoyed our discussion last night. It was most interesting." Lydia cocked her head at him in an enchanting pose.

Fanny handed him the tea she had poured, along with a glance that spoke volumes in warning. "Yes, Lydia and I were just discussing the Greeks."

John tried to overlook Fanny's caution. He knew his pet topic had dominated the conversation last night. He was not going to make that mistake again. "I think there was enough said about the Greeks last night. Today we can talk about something else."

"The Romans?" Lydia asked with a wicked twinkle in her eyes.

"No, the Egyptians."

"Perhaps the . . . the . . ." Her voice trailed off as she struggled to think of another civilization.

Cecil attempted to help. "The Assyrians, or the Babylonians, or the Sumerians. There are many ancient societies we could discuss. Some of them existed closer to home than the Mediterranean." He hitched his chair forward. "For instance, the Angles and the Saxons once ruled England, until the Normans conquered the land in 1066."

For the first time, John understood the glazed look that often overcame his own listeners. "History was well covered last night. I think the ladies would prefer a more recent topic."

Cecil's shoulders drooped, and he contemplated his teacup.

"We were discussing fashion just before you arrived," Fanny said.

Fashion was not his forte, but if Lydia preferred to converse about it, he would struggle gamely. "Your dress is quite pretty," he told her. Ladies liked compliments.

Lydia smoothed a hand down her lap, removing imaginary wrinkles. "Thank you, your grace. I had it made in London."

"The London seamstresses are so much more talented than our country locals." Fanny picked up her teacup and sniffed.

"It is true that the London dressmakers are very skilled," Lydia said. "Of course, many of the French émigrés settled there when they fled. The French do know fashion. Fanny will want a wardrobe designed by them when she reaches the city."

"If I ever do," Fanny muttered.

"I would be happy to give you the names and addresses of those I would recommend."

Overwhelmed by all the information, John said, "That is most kind of you."

To Fanny, Lydia said, "This past summer, dresses with a square neckline were considered quite de rigueur, while trains have pretty much disappeared."

Fanny twitched the small train of her morning dress out of sight. "It does no good to discuss what the fashion was last summer. I dare not follow its dictates. It's next Season's standards I must worry about. I do hope to reach London in plenty of time to have my wardrobe sewn."

John did not want to hear Fanny's complaints. "There is no reason to anticipate problems. You will have a perfectly wonderful Season."

"I never dreamed how wonderful the Season would be," Lydia put in. "Fanny, it is much more than we imagined. The parties, balls, and routs fill the days. There is something new every day."

"You enjoyed it, did you, Miss Grenville?" John asked.

"There is so much to do that the constant activities can eventually wear on one's spirit. I should not say this, but it was good to return to the quiet of Essex."

Her smile at him was very sweet—too sweet. He distrusted it. Would a practiced belle such as Lydia truly prefer the peace of the countryside to shining among the society's stars? Perhaps his very recognition of her coquettish ways protected him from their effect. "But you are eager to return to London?"

"Perhaps." Her smile did not diminish. "Fanny and I always thought we would go together."

"*You* have been," Fanny snapped.

"I can help you navigate society's shoals."

"That is more properly the role of my chaperone."

"I meant I would help as a friend," Lydia said. "I would never presume to interfere with his grace's judgement of your care."

John set his teacup down with precision. He did not like this Lydia who deferred to his every opinion, voiced or not. He was correct. That kiss had been just a momentary aberration, exploding when his guard was down. "A wise man listens to the opinions of those more experienced than he. I appreciate your offer of help."

She kept smiling at him, even as her call drew to an end. The sense of loss growing within him had nothing to do with the polite words of departure. It was true. His Lydia-of-the-woods was no more. That nymph lived only in the forest. This Miss Grenville would possess no power over him.

He stood when she did. She thanked them for the tea and curtseyed very low and very elegantly to him. Her beauty could not be denied, but he would not let his emotions fall into passion in her presence again. He was proud of his control.

Although when she left the room, a cloud seemed to overshadow his vision.

"She's changed," he said.

"Changed?" Fanny asked.

He had not meant to speak aloud. "Miss Grenville. She seems different."

"Different? From when?"

John waved her questions aside. "She's not the same." He turned to Cecil. "Come, I doubt we are done with that report."

With the loss of his woodland nymph obscuring his spirit, John returned to his library with his cousin in tow.

Chapter Seven

The common room of the King's Crown Inn shook with the boisterous laughter of the men who came this evening to forget their troubles in drink and jovial company. It took three running barmaids to fill the shouted orders and answer the suggestive sallies with witty responses.

Sitting in a corner, Ben sipped his mug of ale, watching the activity but not participating. He had overseen the care of the horses currently housed in the stable and had stopped in for his regular drink before going out to see Meg. Men who worked hard and enjoyed their drink filled the room with merriment.

"Come join us," shouted one of the laborers clustered around the wooden center table.

Ben shook his head. "Not tonight."

The rambunctious crowd did not try to change his mind. Unlike many of the men here, he limited his drinking to one mug, carefully nursed. Smug satisfaction filled him. He did not intend to waste *his* pennies down his throat. His savings were growing. Someday he would have an inn of his own, where other men spent their coin.

Life was good. Not only did he have money but he had a good girl he could call his own. She used the skills that made her so pretty to put herself ahead. A ladies' maid was a fine, respectable position. He liked ambition in a woman.

Meg deserved the best in life. She was smart and pretty. He was lucky to have found both in one girl. That she cared for him, too, well, that was just more his luck. Yes, life was good.

He drank another swallow of his ale, feeling it slide smoothly down his throat. A fair quality. He wouldn't mind stocking it at his own inn.

During their last meeting, Meg had agreed to slip out of the manor to see him tonight. He traced a circle on the table as he waited for the time to pass until he should depart. He had seen her two nights ago when the gentry had all been busy at dinner. Imagine a dinner lasting over three hours! That was some feast the Grenvilles served for the duke. Not that he was complaining. No, sir, not he. Meg and he had put that time to good use, kissing and cuddling.

Ben looked forward to their time together—even if it lasted for only a short while. It was time to go. If he was early, he would wait for her. She shouldn't be alone along the road.

He gulped the last of his ale and pushed back from the table. He waved to the two men who called out their farewells before he strode out the inn's door.

The October chill was scented with the fires burning in the town's hearths. A light wind wafted from the docks to his right, bringing with it the smell of the sea. A group of men loitered down the dockyard road. Sailors, most likely. Ben frowned and tugged his coat closed. Then he lowered his head as he trod the familiar road leading out of town.

He didn't like the dockyards. Sailors were good for the money they freely spent and not much else. Ben had no desire for adventure or róving the world. He was of good land-loving English stock. He intended to wed a good English girl and raise up a passel of good strong English lads.

Lost in his plans for the future, Ben made good time down the road. It wasn't long before he was striding through the countryside with its broad hedgerows and stone fences that muffled the night's sounds against their earthen edges. He felt his chest expand, glad he was the only one on the road. The normal traffic of the day was stabled for the night. Beneath his feet, he heard the soft crunch of dead leaves. An owl hooted. Moments later the final terrified scream of its victim cut through the dark. Ben shivered.

The silence that followed seemed to blanket the night. For the first time, he noticed the heavy quiet of the darkness. A sinister quiet. The hairs curled and stood up on the back of his neck. Something else was out there. Something that hunted like the owl. Something predatory.

His steps slowed. His eyes strained to pierce the darkness ahead. The moon was up, but clouds scudded across it, dimming its crescent light. Maybe he should turn back. He knew ghosts did not exist, but he also knew not everything could be explained by reason. A man did not succeed by acting foolishly. Not if he was careful—and Ben was always careful.

He turned around. As if summoned by the darkness, a group of men stretched across the road. Were they ghosts or flesh? Ben didn't care. Without hesitation, he spun back and raced down the road. His feet pounded against the dirt, and he gulped in air like a horse whipped to a speeding frenzy. Behind him, he heard the thundering of many feet.

He recognized them. They had followed him from the docks. Were they out for money or mayhem? Ben carried no money on him. As he ran, Ben thanked the good Lord that his coins were safely hidden away under a stone by the big oak. If they caught him, they'd get not a farthing for their trouble.

He tripped over a stone and stumbled. The men were closing in. Ben cared for horses, he didn't run with them. He didn't have their speed. Why did the men chase him with such determination? Surely they could see by his clothing he wasn't good for robbery.

His foot slipped in a rut. He ignored the wrench. He suddenly realized what they were. A press gang! Men who hunted men to work the ships of the British Navy. Experienced sailors were preferred, but any man of whole limbs would do.

Ben pushed his two legs to keep running. His arms pumped, grabbing for every inch of road. He wouldn't be caught. He wasn't a sailor. He didn't belong on the sea. He was a landlubber, and he raced to stay on the land.

The lane was dark, and the moonlight treacherous. Another rut rocked his steps. His ankle twisted again. The momentary pain caused him to slow. It was enough to betray him. A hand grabbed his shoulder, yanking him backward. Then another gripped his arm. His feet slipped from under him.

"No!" Ben cried. "Not me!"

He swung out wildly. His fist connected with something. Then other fists rained down upon him until he surrendered with bowed head, blurry vision, and bleeding mouth.

He was caught.

Lydia let her fingers trail listlessly over the keys of the piano. She should be practicing her pieces, for a lady must keep up her skills, but every sweet ballad she played ended up sounding as mournful as a dirge. This afternoon she wore her favorite blue sprigged dress, the one she had worn on that first afternoon when she'd met "Alexander." She sighed. He would not see it today.

It was now the fourth afternoon since Winterbourne had dined at Grenville Manor. Three days since she had gone to the woods full of anticipation and met no one. Three afternoons since taking tea with Fanny and attempting to charm him as if he were a London beau.

Yesterday morning she had gone to the clearing, attempting to keep the slightest whiff of hope alive. The autumn wind had scattered both the leaves and her dreams. Forced at last, she admitted the truth she wanted to deny.

He was not coming back.

She would meet him only in the approved social settings, such as tea with Fanny, dinners, and other county parties. That magical time they had shared was truly gone.

She plunked at the keys, not following any melody, only the flyaway direction of her thoughts. She could have called at the castle again this afternoon, except her mother wanted her to stay home in case callers came to the manor.

"Besides," her mother had pointed out, "it is not seemly to be constantly visiting at the castle. Overeagerness can cause a suitor to shy away just as too much reticence can freeze a man's interest."

Her mother was correct. The proper approach was what she needed. She had begun all wrong there in the woods. It had led to that kiss, from which she had built dreams of the future, dreams of being a duchess, of making the brilliant match she had been raised to accomplish. She could still have that future, but now she would follow society's prescribed rituals.

So far, no one had called this afternoon. From her vantage point in the drawing room, Lydia had an excellent view of the drive. No carriage crunched the gravel beneath its wheels.

Suddenly she sat up. A dark figure ran up the drive in a stumbling gait. Lydia narrowed her eyes. Something made her think she should recognize the person. Then she gasped.

It was Meg!

Why was her maid running up the drive? Lydia would have sworn the girl was working upstairs, mending, or ironing, or doing some other such task.

Excitement quickened Lydia's blood. What had happened? She started for the door, intending to intercept the maid when she entered the house.

About to cross the hall, she paused. Of course, Meg would not come in through the front door. Most likely she would return the way she had left, through the kitchen or one of the side doors. No matter how Meg entered, she would still end up in Lydia's room. Lydia would meet her there. She would wait a few moments, thus giving the maid time to resume her position.

After a handful of seconds, Lydia rushed upstairs and found Meg pacing around the bedroom. She made no pretense at working, so lost in her thoughts that at first she did not notice her mistress's arrival.

"What is wrong?" Lydia asked, concerned about the distress writ plain upon the maid's face.

"It's Ben, miss. My Ben. He's taken. And I'll never see him again." Tears coursed down Meg's face. She made no effort to dash them away. "What will I do? My Ben's gone."

Lydia blinked at the onslaught. Ben? Meg's beau? The one who wanted to own an inn? "Gone? Where did he go?"

"To the ship," she wailed. "He's gone."

"Calm yourself, Meg. Take a deep breath. I don't understand what you're trying to say."

Quaking with anguish, Meg gulped in several breaths. Lydia placed her arm around the girl's shoulders and led her to the bed. "Sit and tell me what happened to him."

With tears and trembling, Meg told what she knew. Last night she had slipped out to meet Ben at their favorite spot, under the big oak tree growing at the corner where the drive met the road. She had waited and waited, but he never came. Understanding that emptiness, Lydia hugged the maid. Knowing that Ben would have been there, Meg had raced to town after luncheon today to see him. Only he wasn't at the stables.

"He's been pressed into the Navy," Meg wailed. "And I'll never see him again."

With fear in her stomach, Lydia tried to reassure the girl. "You don't know that."

"Yes, I do, miss. The men at the inn told me. They knew. It was all over town. Ben was taken last night. I'll never see him again."

"You mustn't say that. He will come back."

"No, he won't." Meg twisted her skirt in her hands. "Ben isn't a sailor. He'll be killed by a cannon, or drowned, or take sick, or . . . or . . ."

The future was too dark for her. Sobs claimed her, reddening her eyes. Her skin mottled to a splotchy pink. She had twisted wrinkles into her skirt with the strength of a pleating iron. Her maid's grief frightened Lydia. She slid off the bed and began to pace.

"There must be something we can do to get him back."

"There's nothing. Nothing. He's gone."

"Nonsense. He's not dead," Lydia snapped. Fear forced her to be practical. "We must think. Do you know where he is?"

Meg sniffed. "They already have him on the *Gallant*. It sails tomorrow morning with the ten o'clock tide."

"Then we shall have to get him off before then," Lydia declared with more conviction than she felt.

"How?"

"I don't know, but my father will. We'll ask him."

For the first time, a glimmer of hope lit Meg's face. "Oh, I pray he can."

"Come, we must go to him now. There isn't much time."

Lydia found her father by the corral, discussing a horse's leg with his groom.

"Keep rubbing that liniment on his leg," her father said. "It seems to help reduce the soreness."

The groom touched his forelock. "Yes, sir."

Josiah turned to Lydia. "What are you doing out here? The stable yard is no place for a lady. I thought you were entertaining callers."

"No one called today."

"That's disappointing—"

"Papa, I need your help." Lydia interrupted, not wanting to discuss something so trivial as society's doings now.

Concern instantly crossed his round face. "What's wrong, puss?"

"It's Meg who's in trouble."

With a sharp look, her father turned to her maid. "Trouble?"

"Not like that, sir." The maid sniffed. "My Ben, he's been impressed by the Navy."

"Who is Ben?"

Lydia intervened. "Ben is her beau."

"You've been seeing a man?" her father asked Meg.

"Papa, that doesn't matter now. What's important is that he's been impressed. We have to save him."

"Impressed?" He focused on his favorite issue. His stride lengthened, and Lydia had to skip to keep pace. "Those gangs are everywhere. They are a disgrace to the notion of England as a freedom-loving nation."

"Yes, Papa." Lydia clung to his arm, making him face her. "The gang captured Ben last night and put him on a ship, the *Gallant*. It sails tomorrow morning. You have to get him off."

"Get him off?"

"Yes, Papa. He can't be a sailor. He wants to own an inn someday."

"I'm sorry about that, puss, but he's going to be a sailor now."

"There must be something you can do."

His hands were gentle on her shoulders. "I can't, puss."

"No!" Meg cried. She ran in front of him and knelt with her arms outstretched in pleading. "Please, Mr. Grenville. You must save him. Ben isn't meant to be a sailor."

Josiah lifted her to her feet. "Believe me, if I could help, I would. There's nothing I can do."

"No?" Meg asked in a small, faraway voice.

"No," he said. "It takes a man of great influence to go against the Navy. I don't have that kind of power. I'm sorry."

Meg did not wail. At this final dashing of her hopes, she was beyond speech. She turned and walked back to the house with the stiff gait of a wooden puppet.

Watching her, Lydia felt sympathy welling up. To lose someone you loved and never even say farewell . . . "Papa, is there truly nothing you can do?"

He shook his head. "I'm afraid not, puss. This impressing of men causes a great deal of tragedy. The Navy protects England's shores and needs men to fill those ships. However much I despise the gangs' methods, they are on the King's business."

"The King's business," Lydia repeated.

"Yes, puss."

Lydia stepped away from her father. "It is wrong to steal someone's future from them. You always said so."

"I wish I could help."

"I know, Papa. It's not your fault." She started for the stable. "I need the carriage readied. I must make a call."

"A call? It's rather late in the day for that."

"It's important. I must go now."

"Where are you going?"

"To the castle."

If anyone had dared to ask, John would have said he had spent the day reading his biography of Alexander. The thick volume certainly lay open in the center of his desk, surrounded by the stacks of reports from Cecil and the even higher stacks of invitations from the county's matchmaking mamas. He had no difficulty ignoring the piles of paper, but it surprised him that his book held no allure. It was one of his favorites, yet he could not lose himself among its pages.

He knew the cause—Lydia and the kiss they'd shared.

Although it had occurred more than four days ago, he could still taste the sweetness of her lips and feel the softness of her body against his. She haunted all of his waking moments. Even seeing her in the setting of a call did nothing to diminish his memories. She tilted her head just as he remembered. Her voice still wove her enchantment. Her blue eyes still lured him into staying by her side. She tempted him despite his knowing she hunted him for *what* he was and not *who* he was. He didn't need Fanny's incessant warnings nipping in his ears. His experience with Lydia had revealed her true intentions. At both the dinner and the follow-up call,

Lydia had sought to charm him, but her tone was false. He had correctly read her predatory gleam.

Disgusted at his continuing to think of her, John slammed the biography closed, disturbing the sanctuary of his book-lined retreat. He stood and pushed back his chair so hard it caught on the rug and fell backwards. Annoyed, he righted the chair. It was no good taking his anger out on inanimate objects. They were not the cause of his ill humor. He paced to the window overlooking the lawn, which ended in the stone fence demarcating the castle grounds from the forest. He forced his gaze away from the view.

He was a student, trained to think and reflect. Previously he had used his skills to study the ancient Greeks, their phi-losophy, their arts, the lives of their great men. Yet it seemed that once his mind was trained to wrestle with a topic, it could not stop. He wanted to put Lydia—no, Miss Grenville—out of his thoughts. He wanted to forget the woman she was. The huntress—and the wood nymph. For-getting the huntress would also mean letting go of his Lydia-of-the-woods. She was both. And thanks to their kiss, she had become a part of him.

He could not forget her. She was entwined in his memory, impossible to banish. She had bound him to her with her siren ways. Maybe time could lessen the impact of her spell. He could only wait and see if the passage of days helped. But how would he do this when he must continue to meet her on a regular basis at the local society events?

Groaning, he clutched his head. He was not going to es-cape her. Every time he saw her, he would be reminded of the passion that had ignited between them.

The only way to free himself of her influence was to leave. He must depart Winterbourne Castle. Say farewell to

Cecil and his incessant demands, to Fanny's continual complaining, to the woods and Lydia's enchantment.

Where would he go?

His gaze fell upon the biography of Alexander still lying on his desk. Greece. The land where order ruled. Where white temples stood serene in green groves. Where the great questions about the meaning of good and what is virtuous were debated by the heirs of Socrates and Plato. A place where his mind could find peace from the torment within.

He must go—and quickly. Once beyond Lydia's aura, his life could return to the peace he had once known at Oxford. If he must be the duke, then he would choose the path of his life, and he chose that of the scholar.

A knock sounded sharply against his library door, interrupting his thoughts. His brow lowered. Who disturbed him? It was exactly such demands that he would leave behind.

"Enter," he called.

The door opened, framing Cecil, dressed in his plain brown clothes and carrying his ever-present stack of papers. John's momentary annoyance disappeared. Here was more proof that he chose the right path. His secretary was perfect for his needs.

"Come in, come in." John impatiently waved his cousin forward.

Surprise widened the man's eyes. "Did you want to see me?"

"Yes. I have an urgent matter for you to attend to."

"An urgent matter? For you?" Pleasure lit his face.

John motioned Cecil toward the chair placed before the desk.

Cecil sat with hesitation. "What can I do for you, your grace?"

John rested one hip on the corner of the desk. "I am going to Greece," he announced.

"Greece! When? Why?"

"As soon as possible." He did not intend to reveal the why of his trip to anyone.

"For how long? What will you do?"

"I do not know how long. For whatever the length of time it takes to visit the sites I have long dreamt about." If he must be a duke, then he would take complete advantage of the opportunities the rank bestowed.

Cecil strove to master himself. "But the estates—what will happen to them?"

"They will have the best of care." John leaned forward and placed his hands on his cousin's shoulders. "Yours."

"Mine?" Cecil's hand shook and the papers rustled. "What do you mean?"

"I mean you will be in charge. I entrust everything to your care—the castle, the estates, all of it." With a sweeping gesture that encompassed more than just the library, John said, "Under your management, I know it will thrive."

"But I am not the duke."

"True." There was honest regret in John's voice. "But you will have all of the power—the ability to have things run the way *you* prefer. I will have the legal papers drawn up to give you the authority."

Shock spread across Cecil's face. He managed to stammer, "This—this is a tremendous, a generous offer—a gift. I shall be in your debt forever, your grace. I will be your good and faithful steward for the rest of my life."

Cecil pressed his hand to his heart as he promised, "I swear you can depend upon me to care for all those you have placed in my care. They shall not want, and you shall not regret this day."

The secretary's overwhelming gratitude embarrassed John. "Well, yes, then, I suppose the first thing to do is contact the solicitors. I want to get to Greece as soon as possible." *And far away from Grenville Manor and the surrounding forest.* The quicker the better, so no more memories would haunt him.

"Yes, your grace. Immediately, your grace." Cecil stood and dropped some of his papers. He snatched them from the floor, not caring that he crumpled them in his grasp. "I shall attend to your request first thing, your grace. The fastest ships, the most comfortable inns, I will schedule it all."

John was amused in spite of his own concerns. "Didn't you have something you wanted to discuss with me?"

"It is not important, your grace."

"Surely those papers indicate something of great import. You came to see me for a reason."

"It can wait for later," Cecil assured him, already heading for the door.

Or until you are in charge, John mentally finished. It didn't bother him at all to leave his cousin in command. He could be trusted. With a shrug, John knew he would not miss the interminable dull reports. "Very well, then. We'll let it wait."

A subdued knock sounded on the door. Cecil opened it to reveal the butler, Scott.

With his shoulders held back and a disapproving pinch to his lips, the man extended his silver tray toward John. "Miss Grenville has called, your grace. In person. She asks to speak with you."

Glancing at the tray, John saw the white card with Lydia's name engraved upon it. She was here! To see him. But why? What had happened? His heart did not want to debate the possibilities. It sprang upward as if discharged from a slingshot. "I will see her. Where is she?"

Chapter Eight

"*M*iss Grenville, what is it? What is wrong?" The duke strode into the drawing room, concern written on his face.

Lydia's breath caught in her throat. She had done the right thing in coming to the castle. He would help. She knew it. He looked so noble, so dignified, a true knight even if he was not clad in shining armor.

No longer dressed in his shabby clothes from the forest, he now wore his black superfine coat tailored to fit and breeches designed to display his legs to an advantage. His hair was charmingly disarrayed; his valet must have worked quite hard to obtain that romantic look. He appeared like the duke he was—and he was hers.

Or he would be soon enough.

At this moment, though, she must remember why she was here. Lydia rose to sketch a flowing curtsey, which contrasted to the jerking motion that Meg bobbed. The maid then resumed standing behind Lydia's chair.

"Your grace," Lydia said, "thank you for seeing me."

He bowed his greeting in return and sat. "It is late for an afternoon call. What brought you here?"

Lydia settled back on the chair, making sure her skirt fell in graceful folds. "I need your help."

"You shall have it."

His promptness caused a warm glow to kindle within her. It was quite gratifying how quickly he agreed to her wishes. "Last night, my maid's beau was impressed. He needs to be rescued."

"Your maid's beau?" The quizzical eyebrow he raised in Meg's direction showed his surprise that such a person existed.

Lydia swallowed. She had started badly. Meg should not have a beau. Most maids would be turned off if such a situation was discovered. "Yes. It is foolish to attempt to stop the heart's path."

"Following that path can lead to a passion of greater strength than one realized," he observed.

Was he remembering their kiss? Its passion still stirred within her like a storm rumbling in the distance. Far away, but never overlooked. She swallowed again and pasted on her most charming smile. "Very true, but regardless of how I manage my servants, the fact remains her beau has been impressed."

"I regret to hear that, but what do you want me to do?"

"I want you to get him back."

He blinked at her bluntness. "Well, certainly I will do all in my power, but specifically what can I do?"

"Use your power," Lydia said. "You are a duke."

"I do not understand."

Bewilderment wrinkled his brow, and she understood. He truly did not comprehend what influence his rank bestowed. He did not know what authority his wishes possessed. She would help him, willingly. "I asked my father for help, but he explained there is nothing he can do. Without rank, high rank, he does not have the power to free Ben Stark."

"Ben Stark? Is that his name?" When Lydia nodded, he said, "I understand you want me to use my rank, but how?"

"You could demand that Ben be released from the ship."

Meg broke into their conversation. "Please, your grace, you must save him. Ben is not meant to be a sailor."

Rather than taking offense at this gross breach of manners, the duke spoke gently to the girl. "I am willing to try."

With desperation in her tone, Meg continued, "He is on the *Gallant*. It's supposed to sail tomorrow morning at ten o'clock. There's not much time. Please, your grace, you must help."

Lydia could hear how close the girl was to hysterics, and she did not want to subject Winterbourne to them. "Hush, Meg. He will help. He's promised." Turning to the duke, she suggested, "You could go to the harbor master. He should be able to get Ben off the ship. Or perhaps you could persuade the *Gallant*'s captain."

"You have it completely figured out," he said. "You know exactly what I should do."

"I am only applying simple logic to a problem, much like the Greeks would do," she added, attempting to appeal to his interests. "The harbor master or the captain seems the proper person to approach."

"Yes, they do."

His attitude puzzled Lydia. He relaxed on his chair with his hand brushing his cheek, and his hazel eyes filled with a speculative glimmer. For the first time since she had arrived, a frisson of alarm shivered within her. Perhaps he was not so easily swayed toward her desires as she had hoped. She attempted to repair any cracks in her allure. "Of course, I only offer suggestions. Your grace will determine the correct method."

"It is up to me. After all, I am the duke," he agreed. His hand dropped away from his face. "Tell me, Miss Grenville, do you always know the correct way to make men do your bidding?"

Startled, she went rigid on her seat. "I beg your pardon?"

He glanced at Meg still standing behind Lydia. He stood and offered her his arm in escort. "Come with me."

Although uncertain, Lydia rose. One did not disagree with a duke. "Where are we going?"

"Just to the other side of the room," he said, suiting action to words and leading her away. "I do not want your maid to overhear us."

Excitement replaced hesitation within Lydia. In London, she had perfected the art of flirting under a chaperone's nose. "Ben is her beau."

"I am well aware of that." Once in the corner of the drawing room beneath the portrait of the second Duke of Winterbourne, he halted and faced her. "So, Miss Grenville, you wish to use my influence at your command."

"Not for me, your grace. For my maid." Despite her demure answer, every fiber of her being concentrated upon him. His voice was so low, she had to stand close to hear him. His face filled her vision. All she could see was his hair, his eyes, and his lips.

He brushed a nonexistent speck of lint from his sleeve. "It is *you* who are making the request."

"Yes, I am." She hesitated. His unyielding stance and his probing gaze caused that frisson of alarm to widen into a crack. This did not seem the promising prelude to a flirtation.

"If we are to trade for my influence, surely there is something you could offer in return."

Alarm and excitement blossomed within her. She smoothed her skirts before lifting her face toward him. "What could I offer you, your grace? I am only a girl. I own no possessions but my dowry."

She let the statement of the asset linger on the air with its implied suggestion of her hand in marriage.

"You are always so confident," he said. "So certain of yourself, no matter how you affect those under your spell."

She considered tossing her head in a coquettish manner, but the desperation lurking in his eyes gave her pause. Under the portrait of the second duke, she saw he was not the man she thought she knew. Instead, he resembled his ancestor. Not in the style of dress, for of course the duke in the painting was clad in hopelessly outdated fashion; no, the resemblance existed in the tilt of his head and the set of his chin. No warmth now was evident in the hazel eyes of either the subject of the painting or the man before her. "Alexander" had vanished. It was the Duke of Winterbourne who stood before her.

"Whom else could I turn to for help?" she asked.

"Yes, we must never forget I am a duke." He squared his shoulders. "Very well, then. If I am to free Ben, you must do something in exchange."

The very air seemed to hold its breath. "What?"

"Kiss me."

Exhilaration spiked through her. "Now? Here?"

"If I asked you to, would you?"

She glanced back at Meg.

His gaze followed hers, and his jaw tightened. "No, you are correct. Not here. Later, in the forest."

She did not even attempt to refuse. She was so close to her goal, but a girl did not win a man by appearing permissive.

Holding up a gloved hand, she said, "You must first get Ben off that ship and back to my maid."

"I will do it."

His gaze fastened on her face, and she could not help focusing upon his lips. A pale color, just the perfect size. She remembered their strength and their tenderness. His outer trappings might be different, yet a connection still beat between them. He remembered it and so did she. Indeed, it would be too easy to kiss him again.

"Lydia!" Fanny's voice broke in. "I didn't know you had called."

Lydia straightened. "Fanny, I am glad to see you."

"I am surprised to see you," she said. "Why are you calling so late? It is nearly the dinner hour." Her gaze flicked from Lydia to the duke.

He said, "I will not be here for dinner. Have the cook pack me something light to eat. Quickly. I have not a moment to waste."

"Not here? Why not?" Fanny asked.

"I don't have time to explain." When she began to protest, he held up a hand. "Fanny, tell the cook what I requested. I must have my carriage readied."

"But what is happening?" the girl wailed. "Tell me what is occurring."

Ignoring her, he turned to Lydia, his hazel eyes serious as they connected with hers. "I will bring Ben back. I promise." He spoke as if he were a medieval knight making a vow to slay the dragon or defeat the enemies besieging the castle.

She lifted her head. "And I will keep my promise, too."

No smile lifted the corners of his lips. He nodded briskly in acknowledgment and then strode out of the drawing room, his shoulders back and his spine straight. Lydia did not even have time to curtsey farewell. The forgotten etiquette did not bother her. He was her champion.

"What promise?" Fanny asked. "Will you please tell me what is happening?"

Lydia prepared to deal with Fanny's demands. Whatever she told the girl, she knew she would not reveal the promised kiss. Smugness filled her. Despite his unyielding stance and short tone, he was not indifferent to her. No man could be and still demand a kiss in repayment.

It took longer than John expected before his carriage was ready and he was jolting over the night-shrouded road toward town. He had managed to bring along a piece of bread and a slice of roast beef, thinking food would give him the strength he needed to complete his mission. Yet now it lay like a lump in his belly and clogged his throat, despite the wine he had drunk to wash it down.

The bread had been thick, and he had probably not chewed it sufficiently before swallowing. He swallowed again.

The lump remained at the back of his throat.

He was on a quest, and he was scared. What if he failed?

He rode in the coach with his crest painted on the door. A groom and two footmen accompanied the driver. John had ordered the most ostentatious equipage for this trip to town. He intended to impress. Yet deep down, he knew the outer trappings were there as much to reassure himself of his position as to overawe those he encountered.

Pushing himself forward, demanding his way, were not actions taught a second son. His brother, George, had grown up knowing the dukedom was in his future. He had learned the ways of command from the cradle. John had not.

"I've studied the career of Alexander the Great," John told

himself. "If anyone pushed himself ahead, it was he. I can emulate him."

Saying it aloud made the statement stronger. Very well, then. He would practice his speech.

John drew a deep breath and said, "I am the Duke of Winterbourne. I am here to obtain the release of a man wrongly impressed last night. His name is Ben Stark, and he is on the *Gallant*. Please bring him here."

He considered the speech. Too long. It made him sound like a petitioner. Even though he was, it was the wrong gambit. The Duke of Winterbourne never begged. He commanded. He must remember that.

If he concentrated on that, maybe he could forget the kiss he had demanded in payment from Lydia. Why had he requested that? Their first kiss dominated his thoughts. What had possessed him to attempt to repeat it? He knew the answer. The second kiss was an inspired experiment. A second kiss would banish the effects of the first because he would be prepared. Surprise had caught him unguarded before. This one would lay all his unruly emotions to rest. Was that not what he hoped?

The carriage wheels jolted as they left the dirt road and encountered the cobblestone paving of the town street. He was getting closer. Soon he would be there. He must think of how to save Ben. The success of his quest meant he would receive her boon—an incentive he desperately craved for his peace of mind.

The carriage pulled up outside a building with a lit lantern hanging by its door. The glow of candles reflected against the drawn curtains of the right window. John watched as one of his footmen climbed down and pounded on the door. It was a very imperious knock.

It got attention. The door opened. A thin man peered out into the dark. "Who's there? What do you want?"

The footman positioned himself so the lantern's light shone upon his livery. "The Duke of Winterbourne will see you now."

As his carriage door was opened and John climbed out, he had to admire the footman's condescension. It was as if the servant held his master's rank. John could act no less authoritative.

"The Duke of Winterbourne! Welcome, your grace." The man bowed so low that John hoped his own knees did not shake, for they were at the man's eye level. It would not do for this man to see John's unease. Holding open the door, the man gestured the way inside. "Won't you please come in, your grace. My name is Robert Thompson, and I am eager to serve you."

"I am glad of that," John said.

The boards creaked beneath John's feet as he entered. The office lay to the right of a small hall. On the shelves, papers were piled messily with thick ledger books interspersed among the layers. The aroma of old tobacco mingled with the salt air of the sea from the nearby docks. A wooden spindle chair sat before a cluttered desk. The man hurriedly wiped the chair with his handkerchief. "Please sit here, your grace, and tell me what you require."

John sat carefully. The chair did not look too strong, but although it wobbled unevenly, its construction was sound. Still, he dared not relax. He faced a new situation. How did one go about using one's rank to influence another?

The man shifted on his feet and certainly appeared eager to please. John could only hope that when put to the test, this reedy-looking man would be capable of performing the task.

"A man has been wrongly impressed. I am here to see he

goes free." Not a bad statement. Short and succinct, and allowing no sign of his inner apprehension.

"They impressed one of your men? That's very bad. Very bad, indeed."

John hesitated. He did not want to lie and name Ben as one of his household. "The man is not one of mine."

"He's not?"

"No, he's more of a . . . an acquaintance."

"A friend!" Mr. Thompson wrung his hands. "This is terrible."

"Yes, it is. It can be rectified by getting Ben Stark off the *Gallant* and letting him go free." That was a good pronouncement of what he wanted.

"I'm afraid I can't do that, your grace." He twisted his hands so hard water could have dripped from them.

"Why not?" John demanded. "Just row out to the ship and get him."

Mr. Thompson shook his head. "I can't, your grace. I just can't."

"Then who can?"

He shuffled his feet as he thought. "Maybe the harbor master, Mr. Gibson."

"Aren't you the harbor master?"

"No, your grace. Not me." Relief flooded the man's face. "I'm just his assistant. But I'll go get him for you. Right away."

Before John could speak again, Mr. Thompson snatched his hat off a peg and dashed away. The outer door slammed shut behind him, cutting off the sound of his footsteps against the cobblestones. John was alone with only the sound of a ticking pendulum clock. Its steady beat counted out the passing seconds, and he realized he had made a mistake.

He should never have allowed Mr. Thompson to leave the

room without him. Who knew how long it would take for him to find the harbor master? Once found, would the man return to his office with any speed? He might if he knew a duke waited, but if that duke stood right in front of him, there would be no question about the harbor master's speed.

John groaned. He could not sit and wait. Instead, he paced the cluttered confines of the office. What should he do—wait, or attempt to find the harbor master's residence? He lifted the curtain and looked out at his carriage.

The footmen lounged against it, talking to the groom, who sat up in the driver's seat. The coachman was rubbing the ears of one of the horses. The horse shook his head and stamped his foot. His servants and his animals waited patiently. John knew if he stepped outside, they would immediately spring to attention, ready to do his bidding. He could order them to the harbor master's home, but it would take them time to find it. He doubted they knew where it was. Besides, Mr. Thompson was already on his way there. John dared not risk missing the man's return.

Dropping the curtain, John turned back to the office. He must wait. He had no choice. He had caught himself in quite a coil. All because he wanted to banish the memory of a kiss.

The frustration of waiting gnawed at John. He must rescue Ben, if his experiment was to succeed. Although the Greeks were his preferred topic of study, John had also been exposed to Sir Francis Bacon's scientific method during classes. He knew one must repeat an experiment to see if the result changed. His hypothesis stated that the surprise of the kiss was what had produced the explosion of passion within him. He had to believe it was the surprise that caused his emotional storm. He had to believe that when he was expecting it, the kiss would be nothing but a touching of flesh—no matter how soft or how tender. Indeed, the softer and sweeter Lydia's caress was, the better the proof that he had allowed his emotions to run roughshod.

But how long must he wait? The tide would not wait for Mr. Gibson's arrival. When it went out, so would the *Gallant*. John wanted to punch a wall, the desk, or that ticking clock, but fists against inanimate objects would not speed the harbor master's arrival.

Forty-five minutes later, another carriage rattled up beside John's. Peeking through the curtain, John saw a stout man descend from it along with Mr. Thompson. He could only surmise that the harbor master, Mr. Gibson, had appeared. The man tugged his coat into position and approached with a rolling gait that betrayed his life on the sea.

John scooted onto his seat and schooled his face into a mask of impassive haughtiness. Yes, he was the petitioner, but he was also the duke. He must remember the power that belonged to him. He must not let Mr. Gibson confuse him into making a mistake the way his assistant had.

Trailed by his Mr. Thompson, the harbor master entered with a booming, "Welcome, welcome, your grace. I am most honored by your visit." Mr. Gibson bowed deep enough that John could see the bald spot on the top of his head.

"I need your aid," John said, determined not to dally around his purpose. He did not like Mr. Gibson standing over him, but he would not ask the man to sit down. That implied a long session of dispute. He did not have the time to waste.

"Well, now, as to that, your grace." Mr. Gibson straightened and cast a look at his assistant, who shifted his balance uneasily. "There may be some difficulty involved."

From the uneasy stance of Mr. Thompson, John knew the man had already appraised the harbor master of the situation. "What difficulty? I merely want the man released."

"He's already on the *Gallant*. It is due to sail on the morrow."

"I know this. It is why I have come to you. As harbor master, you should be able to expedite Ben Stark's discharge." John kept his voice bored, yet still in control. He wished he had a walking stick that he could rest his hands on while staring at Mr. Gibson. A duke should have such an accessory.

"It is not such an easy matter."

John lifted an eyebrow. "But one well within your capabilities."

Mr. Gibson pulled out a handkerchief and wiped his palms on it. "If I had more time, yes. The matter could be investigated. The facts ascertained."

"An investigation would not reveal more than you already know. This man should not have been impressed. He is not a sailor."

"Not just sailors are needed. The Navy also requires carpenters."

"Ben Stark is a groom at the inn. He cares for horses. Perhaps the Army could use him, but I doubt the Navy has many horses on its ships."

Mr. Gibson patted his face with the handkerchief. "Everything your grace says is true, but I can't get him off that ship."

"Can't?"

"He's on the ship."

"Get him off." John put all the authority he could into his voice, but he feared failure lurked, ready to pounce.

"I have no jurisdiction there," Mr. Gibson explained. "The captain rules on the ship."

John stood. "Then take me to him."

"Now?"

"Yes."

Mr. Gibson gaped before closing his mouth on a gulp. "I need to make arrangements first, your grace. The captain is not ready to receive a duke."

"*I* am ready to receive him. That is all that is necessary." John opened the door. "You only need to find me a boat and the men to row it to the *Gallant*."

"But—"

John interrupted him with a loud sigh. "Mr. Gibson. You do not understand. I want Ben Stark back, and I want him back now." He took a deep breath and felt power surging through him. It was true. He was the duke. He was Winterbourne. He was not going to let this man's petty bureaucratic concerns disrupt his goal. A duke could do as he liked, and others had to conform to his wishes.

With renewed authority, he continued. "Let me give you a piece of advice. You are the harbor master here. I am the Duke of Winterbourne. I am certain I possess some authority over this port." He did not know if the statement was true, but Cecil could discover the facts. "Do you wish to remain in your position?"

"Yes, your grace. Exceedingly so." Mr. Gibson bowed and turned to his assistant. "You heard the duke. Get a boat and rowers. Now!"

Mr. Thompson scampered through the door with the speed of a fox chased by the hounds. John refused to lose the man. To Mr. Gibson, he said, "Shall we go with him?"

Despite his polite words, it was not a request. They followed Mr. Thompson toward the docks. That power still poured through John as if he had drunk a measure of the gods' nectar produced on Mount Olympus.

After some time, Mr. Thompson found a boat and rounded up some men to row it. John climbed aboard with some trepidation and Mr. Gibson joined him. The water seemed choppy to John, and an occasional cold spray struck him from the men's oars. The moon yielded only a half-light, and the lantern in the stern did not pierce the darkness very far. If he had allowed his imagination free rein, John could have believed he was crossing the River Styx. The men looked rough enough to be servants of the ferryman Charon.

He would not be deterred by either imaginary or real obstacles. He would get Ben off that ship, and he would break the spell that Lydia's kiss had laid upon him. If he'd owned a walking stick, he would have stamped it against the floorboards of the boat for emphasis.

It was close to midnight before John climbed the rope ladder that hung over the ship's side and stood on the deck of the *Gallant*. Captain Edward Whittaker was roused from his cabin and, bleary-eyed, bowed his greeting.

Once the purpose of their visit had been explained, the captain was not inclined to release Ben.

"I need every available hand to man my ship," he said, looking at Mr. Gibson for support.

He did not find it. The harbor master spread out his hands in a gesture of conciliation. "Captain, his grace makes a very minor request. Why not please him?"

With his hands on his hips, the captain faced John. "On board this ship, I make the decisions. These are my men."

"Very true," John said, "but this man did not volunteer to serve under you."

"Impressment doesn't bring me the best sailors, but I make do with the materials I have."

"This particular resource I wish to withdraw." John smiled in what he hoped was a mollifying manner. "Come, Captain. You do not need to keep Ben Stark as one of your sailors."

With a harrumph, the captain crossed his arms. "This is my ship."

"Yes, I know you are the commander here." John pulled himself up to display every inch from his height and looked haughtily at the man. "A ship must come to shore sometimes, and politics are played out on land. A duke can be the patron of that ship's captain—or his enemy. If you do this for me, I will be in your debt. A man who wishes to advance in the world would do well not to anger those powerful enough to help him with his career."

Captain Whittaker eyed him truculently. "This man means that much to you?"

"I want him back."

The man hesitated, while John held his breath. Outwardly he maintained an aloof air, yet once again he wished for a walking stick to clutch and help to steady his hands. He had never tried to assert his power in such a raw fashion. Would he succeed? Could he, as a duke, demand that his wishes be fulfilled?

"Very well, then," the captain said. "Take him with you."

"If you will please have him brought up . . ."

With anger apparent in his movement, Captain Whittaker turned to one of the sailors behind him. "Find this Ben Stark and get him off my ship." He glowered at John. "Politics, bah! Give me the sea, where a man's skills are truly measured. Not this skulking for favor that haunts the halls of the Admiralty." He paused in his rant. "I expect you to speak for me there."

John ignored the lack of respect in the captain's speech. "I will remember you, Captain Edward Whittaker."

Dizziness stirred at the periphery of John's awareness. He must maintain his distant air, despite the shock threatening to overwhelm him. A duke could have his wishes satisfied.

Maybe he could break the spell Lydia's kiss had laid upon him. Maybe his life could return to the placid existence it had had that day before he ran into the woods and met an enchantress.

The sun had barely cracked the horizon's edge when the Winterbourne carriage plodded around the large oak tree standing at the corner of the road and up Grenville Manor's drive. Everyone was tired. The horses bowed their heads as they pulled the coach forward. The coachman huddled in his seat, the reins loose in his hand. The other servants swayed to the motion of the carriage and rested their eyes. Only the passengers remained alert.

Ben bolted upright as soon as he spotted the oak tree.

Amusement touched John at his fellow traveler's reaction. "We are almost there."

"I know. I can't believe it, your grace. I'm in your debt forever."

John waved off Ben's gratitude. He'd heard it ever since they'd been rowed back from the *Gallant*, and it wearied him. In fact, his whole body ached with exhaustion. He wanted to lay his head back against the seat and close his eyes, but every time he did so, he discovered that the only part of him that was not completely fatigued was his thoughts.

They raced with images of Lydia. He remembered the way her golden curls rested against her white neck, how her eyes danced when she teased him, and the deftness of her fingers as they sketched with sure skill. Most of all he remembered her lips: their smiles, their full redness, and their sweet taste. Soon he would be free.

Once the rowboat had docked, he could have sent Ben on his way back to the inn but he did not. John wanted Lydia to see his success. He wanted her to know he could rightfully claim her kiss.

So now the carriage rattled up the gravel drive toward Grenville Manor. Anticipation pounded louder along his veins than the sound of the horses' hooves. How would Lydia react when she saw his arrival?

The carriage crunched to a halt. Without regard for protocol, Ben pushed open the vehicle's door and jumped out. "Meg! Meg!" he bellowed.

One of the footmen assisted John from the carriage. Smoothing his coat into place, John saw that the manor continued to drowse in its morning sleepiness despite Ben's summons.

Ben called for his sweetheart again.

This time John spotted a movement at one of the upper windows. A shriek, although muffled by the walls, clearly resounded inside. Barely a moment later, the latches rattled as they were pulled back, and the front door was flung open with a bang. Meg threw herself into Ben's arms. He staggered under the assault but gripped her tightly to his chest.

"Oh, Ben," she sobbed over and over. "I never thought to see you again."

"Meg," he said. His hands tangled in her hair as he kissed her long and deep. She pressed close to him as if she would bond with him like metals in a blacksmith's fire.

Glancing away, John blinked at the sudden extra moisture in his eyes. He had thought so much about Lydia's kiss that he'd overlooked what his successful quest meant to Ben and Meg. Seeing their obvious joy overwhelmed the restraint he struggled to maintain on his emotions.

The creak of a window opening caused him to look up. Lydia leaned out. Seeing her hair still in night braids and a wrapper around her shoulders, John knew she had only just arisen from her bed.

"What is happening?" she called.

With a swagger in his step worthy of the hero Hercules, John strolled until he was beneath her. "I brought Ben back."

Her hand flew to her mouth, covering her lips. "You did? You saved him?"

"I did."

"Thank you," she said. "Oh, thank you. You were the only one who could save him."

"I am glad to be of service," he said, not looking at the couple embracing only a few feet from him.

Lydia's cheeks were warm from sleep and the wisps of hair escaping from their braids lent a softness to her face. Could he read gratitude in her eyes or something more? Though she was too far away for him to see for certain, he nevertheless took a step closer.

"What the devil is going on here?" The booming voice of Mr. Josiah Grenville interrupted. He stood on the steps, with his rose-colored brocaded robe hastily thrown over his night-clothes. The servants hovered behind him.

Meg and Ben disengaged to face him, but Ben's arm remained clasped around her waist. "Good morning, Mr. Grenville," he said.

Mr. Grenville's bushy eyebrows lowered. "Get your hands off my maidservant."

Meg made no effort to leave Ben's embrace. "Begging your pardon, sir, but this is Ben. Ben Stark."

"Who?"

John judged it time he introduced his presence. "Good morning, Mr. Grenville."

"Your grace! What are you doing here? What is happening?"

John both pitied and understood the man's confusion. "This man Stark was impressed by the Navy."

"Don't you remember, Papa?" Lydia called from her window. "I asked you to free him."

"Impressed, you say?" Josiah Grenville's mouth worked as if he struggled with many things to say at once. "Terrible, terrible state of affairs."

"Yes, indeed," John agreed.

"You freed him?"

John modestly bowed his head. "My influence was sufficient."

Lydia's father barked a laugh. "I'm willing to bet it was." He straightened and gestured inside. "Your grace, won't you please come in? I am sure my house can offer you a substantial breakfast."

"Thank you, but no. It has been a long night, and I am fatigued," John said.

Josiah nodded and turned his focus to Ben and Meg. "Well, man, I'm glad you're back, but you can't stand here mauling my maidservant all morning. Be on about your work."

Ben tugged his forelock. "Please, sir, I want to marry Meg."

"Marry her?"

"Yes, sir."

"Please, Mr. Grenville," Meg said. "I don't want to lose him again."

Josiah harrumphed and cast a glance up at his daughter. "Lydia, stop hanging out the window! You are a lady." He looked back at the couple. "I suppose we should have at least one marriage around here. Very well, you have my permission to wed, but I want the banns called. No skulking around or scandal when dealing with the women of my household. Understood?"

Looking at the finger pointing at him, Ben nodded. "Yes, sir. Only what's right and proper for Meg."

"Good." Josiah turned into the manor and saw the servants clustered behind him. "Don't you have work that must be done?" They scattered and he shut the door, leaving Meg and Ben to say their farewells alone.

John looked back up at the window. Lydia had not obeyed her father.

"Will you be calling this afternoon?" she asked.

"No," he replied. "I have been awake the whole night, and I am tired. It will likely take until tomorrow until I am recovered."

She shivered in the morning air's nip and pulled her wrap tight. "It is too cold to sketch today. Tomorrow morning's light will perhaps be better."

A long look full of meaning passed between them. Despite the servants still lingering within earshot, he understood her message perfectly. She would not shrink from her promise. She would repay him with a kiss.

Suddenly the morning seemed brighter, clearer. No rain had fallen, but the stones shone as if washed clean. The birds greeting the sun sang a hymn of joy. The crisp air emphasized the fire now racing through his veins. Tomorrow morning was only twenty-four hours away.

"Good morning, Miss Grenville." He bowed as though he were completing a call, not responding to an assignation, and climbed into his coach.

Chapter Nine

$\mathcal{D}$espite John's best intentions to spend the day sleeping, his body refused to cooperate. It ached with fatigue. Both the bed curtains and the room's draperies were drawn, but the afternoon light still managed to cast a soft glow on his bed. He blamed the sun for the fact that his eyes would not stay closed. They felt gritty, as if the sea salt from the ocean's waves had infected them. He just needed to catch up on his sleep, and then everything would be perfectly ordered in his life.

Except—his spirit refused to work with his agenda.

Whenever he shut his eyes, he saw Lydia as she had appeared that morning, sleep-tousled and looking down on him with admiration. He liked it. He wanted her approval. He just did *not* want himself responding so emotionally when she was near. The next kiss would cure him of that.

Except—even when she was not near, she affected him. He groaned and buried his face in his pillow. What was the matter with him?

He wanted to sleep. All logic said his body should be so weary that the very act of lying in his bed should induce slumber. Between yesterday and last night, he had been awake for more than twenty-four hours. He should not have to work so hard for rest.

It was his mind that raced out of control. It wanted to re-member every look and gesture of Lydia's that morning. And once those had been infinitely analyzed to see if he could read her true feelings toward him, then his mind wanted to scrutinize those times when they met in proper social settings and even those delightful times in the woods. Most of all, the bright rays peeking through the bed curtains reminded him of those sunlit meetings.

Tomorrow her power over him would shatter. He would kiss her. The softness of her lips and the silken feel of her hair would no longer torment him. He would touch her, kiss her, and that would end it. When they broke apart, he would be able to regard her as any other woman. Her spell would be broken.

Tomorrow.

Eventually his mind and body achieved a truce, and he fell into an uneasy doze. When he awoke later, he felt as if he still existed in that half-gray world between waking and sleeping. There was no need to continue to chase sleep. It ob-viously acted like a skittish wood nymph, darting away every time he drew close.

John summoned his valet to dress him for the remainder of the day. After shaving and helping John with his shirt, waistcoat, and breeches, Howard reached for the coat with the frayed cuffs.

John started to shrug into it, but then halted and looked at himself in the looking glass. The coat was his favorite, but it had come from his student days. "Not this coat," he said. "Bring me that black one."

Surprise creased the valet's face. "The black one, your

grace? I had not realized you were invited out for dinner this evening."

"I am not. This coat is just too shabby."

Howard stiffened with offense. "I mended it to the best of my ability, your grace."

John hastened to repair the damage caused by his thoughtless words. "It is not your ability I referred to. You did your best given the state of the fabric. That coat is not the proper attire for the Duke of Winterbourne."

"Indeed, your grace." Satisfaction permeated Howard's voice as he folded the coat and set it aside. John remembered the man had said as much several times before.

Properly clad in the black coat, John saw the looking glass reflect a man who was a duke, suave and sophisticated. He lacked only that walking stick. He must purchase one soon.

"Very good, Howard," John said and left his suite.

He ambled down the stairs toward the drawing room. Hearing female voices, he paused to see if he recognized Lydia's. When he didn't, he peeked around the doorframe. Fanny was pouring tea for Miss Elizabeth Chandler and her mother. The girl giggled at some remark of Fanny's. John shuddered. Her laugh had none of Lydia's lilt. Having no desire to present himself for consumption under the ladies' assessing eyes, he quietly turned away and made for the sanctuary of his library.

Yet shutting its door behind him provided no refuge. Irritation grew. Why was he forced to skulk around to avoid these matchmaking women in his own house? Wasn't a man's home his castle? He even owned a castle and yet must lurk in its halls, forced into a hiding place. He should march right down the corridor and order the women to leave.

But that was rude behavior. Inexcusable. The ladies had done nothing to deserve it. They were only acting according to society's rules in introducing their daughters to his notice. A bachelor duke was fair prey. Yes, a duke could do anything he wanted, even break those unstated etiquette laws, but John did not have the initiative to be so discourteous.

Instead, he settled down to read his favorite book, Alexander the Great's biography. Unfortunately its current section related to the aftermath of his Persian conquests, when Alexander had wed two women on the same day in order to demonstrate his policy of integration between the Greeks and the Persians. These two wives were in addition to the one he'd married several years previously.

John shook his head. How had Alexander done it? John was finding coping with *one* woman a difficult task, let alone adding two more into the mix.

At dinner, he had to contend with only Fanny and Cecil.

Fanny commented, "Once again, we are dining alone."

John selected a piece of chicken from the plate the footman held. "We dined at Grenville Manor only a week ago."

"Yes, a *week ago*," Fanny said. "You are the duke. We could have a much more active social life if only you would accept more of those invitations that constantly arrive."

"You can go without me."

Fanny's snort had no pretensions of being ladylike. "As if anyone wants me around without you. Like yesterday— Lydia called to see you, not me. What did she want?"

"It had nothing to do with what you are implying."

"I would not be too sure," she warned.

Because of the promised kiss in his future, John did not want to think Fanny might be right. "She requested I have a man released from naval impressment. That's all," he explained.

Fanny turned toward him with interest. "There were press gangs around here? Who was impressed?"

"One of the men connected with Grenville Manor. He's been released."

"Amazing! Something actually happened in this benighted countryside." Pushing her place setting askew, Fanny leaned forward. "Tell me more."

"There is nothing more to tell. The man is released, and the incident is over." John sipped his wine, fully aware he was not quite telling Fanny the whole truth. To forestall her further nagging and to completely close the incident, he turned to Cecil. "I have some letters which must be written tomorrow."

"No need to worry, your grace," his cousin said. "I have already completed them."

"You have?" How had Cecil known what he had promised to the harbor master and the captain?

"Yes, I have started inquiries for ships headed to Greece."

"Greece!" Fanny exclaimed. "What about Greece?"

Caught up in Ben's rescue, John had forgotten all about his plans to escape Lydia's influence through travel. "I was thinking of taking a trip."

"While he is gone, I will handle all the estate matters," Cecil proclaimed. "There are many improvements to be implemented in his absence. It is all quite exciting."

Fanny's eyes widened in horror. "If you are in Greece this spring, who will sponsor me for my Season?"

John had not given a thought to his ward's debut. He shifted on his chair. "Even if I am here, I cannot act as your chaperone."

"But I've dreamed of having my ball at the Winterbourne townhouse," Fanny wailed.

"You still can," John said, exasperated. "Whichever aunt oversees your come-out will be quite capable of planning the ball."

"You won't be there. Who wants to come to a ball at a duke's home when the duke is gone?"

"Enough, Fanny," he said, annoyed by her sulks. "I have not left yet."

Alarm leapt into Cecil's face. "You said you wished to depart as quickly as possible. I have already drafted the letters requesting information about ships traveling to Greece."

With effort, John mastered his irritation. "Very good. However, the letters I need written are not about my trip to Greece."

"They're not? What are they, your grace?" Cecil asked. "I will do them promptly so they are completed before you leave."

John had not intended to make his business affairs a topic of dinner conversation, but somehow control of the conversation had slipped away from him. "I want to commend the captain who assisted me last night. I promised I would speak well of him."

"I will see that the Admiralty receives notice of your commendation."

"It seems you had to do an awful lot of work to get this man released," Fanny observed. "She did not make a minor request."

"I was honored to help Lydia," John replied, determined to cut off her probing.

"Lydia!" Fanny exclaimed. "You address her as Lydia?"

John felt the cold fear of discovery grip his heart. "It is her name, is it not?"

"It's very forward behavior on your part. You were just introduced to her last week at dinner. Such action is not like you." Fanny's eyes narrowed as she studied him. "Has the temptress actually snagged your interest? I warned you about her."

"Your disparagement does nothing to help your own reputation," John replied. "From your words, I could conclude you care nothing that a man's freedom has been restored."

"Of course I care." Fanny bit into her roll.

John knew he had temporarily silenced her tongue, but her resentment at her caged state in life still smoldered. If he could, he would send her off on her Season right now, but October was not the month of London social gaiety. Fanny must bear her country rustication a little while longer.

His thoughts of Lydia had betrayed him into the indiscretion of mentioning her name. Soon he would break her spell. Her siren song would no longer haunt him, and he could travel to Greece with a clear spirit. Tomorrow this torment would be vanquished. Tomorrow his soul would be released.

Standing before her open wardrobe the next morning, Lydia pondered her choices. Just what did a girl wear to a kiss? The very word caused Lydia's insides to coil like a tangled skein of yarn. What would it be like to kiss Winterbourne again? Would her heart again beat so fast until she was light-headed? Would the tingle still race over her skin to explode within her like the twisting colors of a prism?

She'd been kissed before. A girl enjoying a Season had many such opportunities. But those happened by chance, during the course of a flirtation. Never had she made a rendezvous for a kiss.

So what did a girl wear to such an occasion?

Many of her dresses were fashioned from the white muslin so appropriate for a girl's debut. A quick glance out the window confirmed that autumn had definitely blown in. The breeze ripped the leaves from the trees and sent them scattering past her window. The late-summer weather, which had blessed the area for the past few weeks, had surrendered to the next season. White muslin was no longer appropriate for this weather.

Her riding habit looked most fetching, but Lydia would be walking to their private place. Choosing her habit would mean a horse should also be selected, or else questions would be raised. That left only her gowns meant for country wear. Did she want to wear the heavier woolens when she had played the fairy princess in the past?

Meg stood by the wardrobe, waiting to dress her mistress, but her attention was directed elsewhere. The maid's gaze focused into space. Her memories filled her, and they were apparently happy ones, if the smile twitching at the corners of her mouth was any indication.

A spike of envy thrust through Lydia. "I will wear the yellow dress today."

Recalled to her surroundings, Meg blinked. "Yes, miss." She pulled the dress out and raised her eyebrows. "It is a very bright color."

"I refuse to say farewell to summer yet."

Perhaps it was too bright for the gray morning, yet her coat would cover most of it. Lydia did not care. She had last worn it when she had called upon Winterbourne for tea. They had chatted companionably about fashion and ancient civilizations. She hoped the dress would provide a subtle reminder of their camaraderie. Capturing an offer from this duke needed every bit of coquetry a girl could muster.

Meg dressed Lydia's hair in the requested simple style. Lydia saw no need to waste time developing an intricate style that would be quickly tossed into a mess by the wind. She did not question the maid's capability.

Lydia wanted to know more about Meg's courtship with Ben. "Did you meet with your beau last night?" she asked.

Meg had assisted at her bedtime preparations, but naturally Lydia had not seen her after that.

The sudden pause in Meg's busy hands told the answer.

"You did!"

Blushing, Meg managed to stammer out her answer. "It wasn't for very long, miss."

Lydia remembered how the two of them had embraced with such obvious passion, and another jolt of envy flashed through her. The affection—no, the love—Meg and Ben displayed could not be questioned. "Have you set the wedding date?" she asked.

"No, we haven't met with the vicar yet." Meg finished pinning the last lock of hair into place and stepped back.

Lydia nodded her approval of the result. "I will miss your skills, once you are married."

"If you like, I will stay on as your maid until your own marriage, miss."

Surprised, Lydia turned on her chair to face the maid. "Will your husband approve of such an arrangement?"

"For you, miss, I would do anything." Meg's hands clutched her skirt. "You don't understand how much I owe you."

Lydia turned away, afraid of the depth of gratitude she saw on the other girl's face. Meg's hysteria had frightened her and made her seek a way to make it stop. That path had led to Winterbourne and her promise of a kiss. Now Meg's gratitude made her feel small.

Lydia held up a hand "You don't owe me. I did very little."

"You persuaded the duke to act," Meg declared. "No one else could do it. You saved my man. I won't forget that, miss. After all, I love Ben. I'd be lost without him."

Lydia fiddled with the brush and comb lying on the table

before her. She did not meet Meg's gaze in the looking glass. "That's a very bold statement."

"Almost losing him made me realize how much he means to me."

"You are a very fortunate girl, then, to marry where your heart leads." She stood and looked at Meg.

The maid's mouth opened as if to reply, then she curtseyed. "Yes, miss, I am."

Uneasy at Meg's open emotion, Lydia went down the hall to breakfast with her parents. What could it mean to love someone so much that making such a public declaration was as natural as breathing? Yesterday morning, Meg had shown no restraint in embracing Ben in front of Lydia, her father, the other servants—even Winterbourne himself. The strength of her maid's passion caused Lydia to shake her head. She refused to envy Meg and the love she had found.

Lydia was a lady. She straightened her posture until a book could have balanced on her head. She had been raised to make a marriage worthy of her dowry and her station. She could sing, she could dance, and she could play card games. She could even draw. She had obeyed all of society's strictures for unmarried girls.

All but one.

And see where tossing aside the rules had led her. She had met a man illicitly in the woods. And she had met him more than once, actually anticipating their time together. Then, a miracle happened. He was a duke, and he wanted her kiss.

Smugness and anticipation mingled within her. Although love was not a requirement for the marriage that fate held in store for her, affection could exist between him and her. It already did. It would be enough. Her parents' marriage had shown her that. The unrestrained passion displayed by Meg and Ben was appropriate only for the lower classes.

She was going to be a duchess. She must not forget her purpose. Passion was her lure to gain the duke. She could not, would not, allow it to overwhelm her plans.

When she arrived at the clearing, he was waiting. He intently watched her approach, and for a moment, Lydia's steps faltered. No longer was he dressed in the shabby coat he had worn during their other forest meetings. Today Winterbourne appeared like the duke he was, in a finely tailored coat and crisp linen. His hands were clasped behind his back, and his chin was lifted so his gaze was directed at her. Standing so straight and tall, he resembled the trees surrounding him, rigid and unbending. The wind only ruffled his hair, leaving his body unmoved.

Chiding herself for her hesitation, Lydia went forward until she stood before him. She had promised a kiss, and she kept her promises.

"Good morning, your grace," she said and made a curtsey worthy of the Court.

He bowed stiffly in response. "You came."

"I said I would." She met his eyes, but could not read the message in them. Should she kiss him immediately? Already the knowledge of their purpose here strummed within her like the taut string of a violin.

"You do not have to kiss me." Desperation tinged his voice.

"I won't break a promise."

She could not pretend their meeting had any other purpose, and his rigid stance showed that neither could he.

He took a deep breath. "It is not the same here now."

"It is only windier now. That's all." She suppressed a shiver as the wind went through her. Perhaps the yellow dress had not been the best choice, but it looked so fine against the brown of her woolen coat.

"No, it is different now. The magic is gone."

"The fairy princess still has her wand." Lydia held up one of the pencils she clutched with her sketchbook. She began to wave it, but he reached out and gripped her wrist.

"It won't work, Lydia."

She looked at his hand holding her arm and felt the strength of his resistance to her charm. "What is it? Why won't you let the magic work?"

Looking into his face, she saw how the bones of his cheeks stood out in stark relief. His eyes were narrowed, and he did not brush away the hair blowing over his forehead.

He said, "We cannot go back to before, to the way it was at the beginning."

His insistence began to frighten her. "Why not? It's still the same place. We are still the same people."

He shook his head with sadness. "We are not the same people. You are—and always will be—Lydia-of-the-woods, but I cannot become Alexander."

"But why not?"

"Because you know me differently—now."

"Oh," she said. She understood. He was the Duke of Winterbourne. Every time she looked at him, or even thought of him, she saw his rank—and he knew it. That was her flaw.

He released her wrist, and her hand dropped to her side. Sorrow filled her for that playful simplicity they had once possessed.

"We cannot go back in time," she said. "You, better than anyone, should know that once knowledge is gained, it cannot be forgotten."

He tried to smile. "Yes. It's the lesson of Pandora's box."

"What's that?"

"Pandora was the woman who opened the forbidden box, releasing the ills trapped within so they could ravage the world."

"Why would she do something like that?"

"Curiosity. She did not know what was in the box. Once released, the evil could not be recaptured, and it existed to plague mankind forever."

Lydia sympathized with Pandora, a woman caught by the unforeseeable consequences of her actions. "Certainly she did not intend to let it loose."

"True. She only meant to take a peek, but you are also right when you say knowledge once gained cannot be forgotten."

She glanced around at the clearing shadowed by the gray sky and the leaves falling from the trees. The wind hummed through the branches and leaves, providing an accompaniment to their conversation, as if it were a musician hired at a party. Its sound was low, yet in its restraint lurked the knowledge that it could burst forth with raging strength.

Lydia turned back to him. "Is this to be farewell, then?"

"What else can it be?"

He was so remote, she had to challenge him. "I will continue to meet you at parties and dances."

"The Duke of Winterbourne will always be honored to encounter Miss Grenville." His face shuttered as if to prevent any hint of his self from escaping. She knew better. The companion she remembered must still live, even if hidden behind that façade he constructed.

"Stop it!" Lydia stamped her foot. "You are the duke, but you are also Alexander. I will prove it."

Lydia grasped him by his shoulders and gazed straight into his eyes. He was determined to lock his emotions away as tightly as if they hid within Pandora's box, but in the depths of those hazel pupils she thought she read a need to escape. For good or ill, she would be his Pandora.

She reached behind his head, feeling her fingers glide through his hair. Pulling his face close to hers, she whispered, "I always keep my promises."

Her lips closed on his fully. Despite the chill in the air, heat ignited between them. She refused to retreat with only a light peck and instead pressed herself against him, seeking, searching. He was not so remote, so distant, as he pretended. She had to find the man she knew he was.

Her eyes remained open. She saw the surprise on his face, and then his gaze locked with hers. And the crack in his mask was there. Loneliness and need reached out to her. Her hands caressed his head, his face, and his shoulders, yet it was her heart that plunged forward, giving and accepting.

"Oh, Lydia," he said. "You *are* an enchantress."

His arms tightened around her and one hand pulled her bonnet off to keep her face close. His fingers ran through her hair, destroying Meg's work. Lydia didn't care. He was all that mattered. He wanted her, needed her. She had known that, planned for it even, but she also needed him, and that surprise shattered her plans to charm him. Passion burst forth. Only the senses of touch and taste ruled in a maelstrom of emotion.

She was lost in the whirlwind, but she was not alone. He was with her. Beside her and before her, with his arms clasped behind her, pulling her close even as she melted into him. His lips moved over hers, hot and strong. Her hand stroked his jaw, feeling the smoothness of his freshly shaved skin. Nothing impeded her. No restraint of polite society lasted before her need and his. She kissed and kissed him, reveling in his touch and his taste.

At last, she drew apart and gazed at him. The wind tugged

a lock of her hair free. She felt its flutter against her cheek and saw it brush his own. It was an oddly intimate caress, as if every fiber of her being wanted to reach out to him. Here, in the woods, the masks were dropped. It was only the two of them. Complete.

She rested her head on his shoulder and studied the curve of his chin, the angle of his nose, and the line of his brow. He was a man unlike any other.

Lydia sighed. "I have never been kissed like that."

The arm he had crooked about her waist tightened. "You overwhelm me. You are my Lydia-of-the-woods who has cast her spell over me."

She snuggled closer, taking pleasure in the feel of his body against hers. Earlier she had thought he resembled one of the trees in rigidity. Now she also realized how strong and sturdy he was, and how his embrace sheltered her.

"Can a duke become enchanted?" she asked.

She felt his body stiffen in withdrawal.

"No, Lydia," he said.

Alarmed, she looked at him. "What's wrong?"

"I cannot allow this charm to work." He disengaged from their embrace. "Your magic is too powerful."

"What magic?" she exclaimed, even as dread laced through her. "It's only a game of pretend. A fairy tale."

He shook his head. "It is not pretend. It's real. So real that I cannot escape it."

They stood scarcely inches apart. She could feel him struggling to shut her out again, to regain that remote stance. She couldn't let him succeed. "Then don't hide from it."

She started to lean closer, but he grasped her shoulders. "Don't, Lydia. You have already proved your point. You can make Alexander reappear, but he doesn't really exist. He is not me. I am Winterbourne."

For a moment, she studied him, and then she lifted her chin. "Yes, you are the duke. You are right. I cannot overlook that fact." She drew a breath in deeply. "But as you taught me with the story of Pandora's box, knowledge—once gained—cannot be forgotten. You will not forget Alexander."

The swift intake of his breath acknowledged her truth.

To hide her face, she bent to pick up the pencils and sketchbook she had dropped. When had they fallen from her hands? She did not know or care, not when the realization of his rejection was billowing up from her heart like smoke from a suddenly extinguished fire.

He stooped to help her. She took the two pencils he held out. With a curtsey, she said, "Good day, your grace."

"Let me see you to the edge of the woods," he offered.

"No." She blinked rapidly, trying to maintain her composure. "The fairy tale began here. Let it end here." She walked away.

Winterbourne watched her go, with her head held high and her step sure. He had failed. He had not resisted her kiss. Instead, he had willingly joined her. Her scent, her touch, her taste, even the memory of their kiss overwhelmed him. He could think of nothing but Lydia.

What of his fine ideas now? What had happened to his scientific method to prove the power of her kiss to be a fluke? He had planned for it. Knowing what he faced, he had considered himself superior to the emotional tempest to follow. Hah! His experiment had blown up as if gunpowder had been tossed onto a fire. She shook him to his very soul. Even knowing that she set her sights on him because of his rank could not dislodge her effect upon him.

He kicked at a stone, watching it roll under some fallen leaves before he headed back to the castle. She was right about knowledge, too. "Alexander" existed. It was the irrational part within him. No matter how hard he sought to tame its chaos through the Greek approach of order and logic, the emotions still erupted.

He could blame Lydia, but he knew she was only the catalyst that had broken the barriers of control he had erected. He was the one who had lost himself to her.

Chapter Ten

*A*fter that kiss, which turned out to be such a disaster for her plans, Lydia seemed to encounter the duke wherever she went. Sunday morning he took his place in his pew in the front row of the church. Two rows behind, Lydia spent the entire service noticing the breadth of his shoulders and the way his light brown hair sculpted the shape of his head. He paid proper attention to the sermon, likely getting more out of it than she did.

When the service finished, Winterbourne greeted Lydia and her parents most correctly. She wanted to convince herself that his attention meant something special, but he also paid his respects to others, including Mary Fisher and Elizabeth Chandler. Still, her attraction to him could not be broken. She was smitten.

Later in the week, when she and her mother went shopping, Lydia spotted the duke in town. He strolled along the street, idly swinging his new walking stick. Her heart paused a beat and then skipped onward at a giddy pace, making her light-headed as he approached.

Once greetings had been exchanged, he inquired as to their purchases.

"Our trip has been most successful," Lydia told him. "I found some fabric for a new dress."

"I am certain it will look lovely on you," he said.

She could tell he spoke thus only from politeness. Had she ever shared a passionate kiss with this man? Away from the forest he seemed such a different person.

Determined to jolt him from his reserve, Lydia tilted her head in a flirtatious manner. "I hope you will like it. Today's fashions are very influenced by the ancient Greeks."

"For the women at least."

"True, the men would look odd in the tunics of that age." She laughed. "Besides, the English climate is too cold for such a style." She exaggerated her shiver.

He cracked a slow smile at her joke. "Have you been studying the fashions from the period?"

"Yes, I have developed an interest in their culture and wish to learn more. You, of course, had the advantage of studying them at university."

"I am quite fluent in reading their language—both the ancient and modern form," he told her proudly. "My conversational ability is weak."

"You should be able to improve that when you go to Greece."

"How did you know about that?"

"Fanny told me when she called on Monday. You must be looking forward to seeing the places you have read about."

"Yes, I am." His eyes looked straight into hers.

The intensity of his gaze unsettled Lydia. "I wish I could see such sights." The wistfulness in her voice was not faked. "The Parthenon, the temples, the groves—to walk where great ideas were born."

"You *have* been studying Greece," he said.

There was a bond forming between them. She could feel it. "It's new to me, but I have discovered its fascination."

"Maybe, someday, you will visit there."

"I hope so." Lydia almost whispered her response.

"When do you depart, your grace?" her mother asked.

The connection between them broke. He blinked, and Lydia remembered they were not in the forest.

"I have not yet set a date. It should be soon." He tapped his walking stick on the cobblestone street, his remote demeanor back in place. "I do need to go. And soon."

With a bow, he resumed his walk, moving at a quicker pace that had his footman nearly scampering to keep up. Winterbourne vanished into the traffic of horses and people crowding the street.

Bereft, Lydia dug her fingers into her palms to prevent her tears from forming. He was lost to her once again, and it hurt. She must not cry. Not here, not out in the middle of a public street.

Her mother also watched him leave. "He would be an excellent match for you. What a fine man!"

"I agree, but what can I do to attract him?" It was a cry from her heart.

"It was clever of you to mention Greece." Her mother placed an arm around Lydia's shoulders. "His absorption in it is well known."

"I didn't mention it only to be clever. The Greeks were a bold and thoughtful people."

"Indeed!" Her mother's eyes widened. "I had not realized they had caught your notice."

"It is true that the duke's interest led to my own reading," Lydia said as demurely as possible. How could she reveal how her interest had developed?

Her mother patted her shoulder. "Very good, my daughter."

"I need more than ancient Greece to attract him."

"We shall continue our social rounds," her mother said. "If you constantly meet him and talk about what he wants, you will bring him up to scratch. Although he is shy, you make him feel at ease."

Remembering their kiss, Lydia did not think that ease was why he noticed her. "Will that be enough to make me stand out?"

"You are a lady. You are also beautiful and dowered. Other suitors are also attracted to you. The duke is an intelligent man. He will notice and will want the prize other men desire. That is the nature of men."

Looking at where the throngs of people crossed his path, Lydia wished she possessed her mother's confidence. She wanted to be a duchess, and she wanted Winterbourne to be her duke. Such a marriage would be the perfect fulfillment of her duty because it matched her desire. If only the task of ensnaring him was not so difficult!

"Come, Lydia," her mother said, interrupting her thoughts. "We should be heading home."

Obediently, Lydia followed her mother back to their waiting carriage, but her thoughts whirled as she struggled to sort out her feelings toward Winterbourne.

Her mother talked about making him feel at ease. There had been ease at the beginning when Lydia had thought he was a ducal secretary, an effortless comfort that had allowed them to talk about Greece and drawing. She played at being the fairy princess, and he joined in. No barrier existed then.

Of course, she had thought him totally ineligible.

It was only when his true identity was revealed that everything changed. After her initial anger, she had realized what an opportunity she had to marry him. She had expected that by building on their forest time, it would be a snap to become his duchess. That first kiss proved affection existed between them—the second, passion. She was trying to be the perfect partner for him. Yet none of her calculations worked. He rejected her. Despite her dowry, her accomplishments, her passion, he resisted the bond that could form between them.

What was she doing wrong? And was becoming a duchess worth all this grief?

The questions consumed her as the coach rolled back to Grenville Manor.

Winterbourne could not escape from her influence. Everywhere he went, she was there. Church, town, even tea in his own castle—Lydia was there.

He expected to encounter her at the evening of dancing and cards held at the Fishers' home. Because their house was not large, the company was select. Lydia was a friend of Mary's, and he was included because he was Winterbourne.

He asked for a dance, along with all the other men who clustered around her. Yet when its time came, he asked if they could sit it out.

"I am not very good with the steps," he confessed.

Agreeing to stroll with him around the room, she unfurled her fan. "I should think a man with your education should have no trouble learning the patterns."

"Learning the intricacies of the Greek language was easier," he said with a rueful smile.

"But you wanted to learn that, did you not?"

"Of course."

"Then you have only to desire to learn dancing and you will." She laughed, a merry sound that made him believe he had just uttered a witticism.

He determined to match her cheerfulness. "You think lack of desire is the only obstacle?"

"Naturally. If you do not want to gain a skill, you never will. Knowledge comes from the desire to learn."

She peeked at him over her fan, flirting with him again. He did not mind. She intrigued him with her statement. He wanted to explore it further.

"That is an interesting argument," he said. "So according to you, knowledge requires desire, which is an emotion. I was taught that knowledge should be based on logic."

"Perhaps, your grace, you were taught incorrectly."

His steps hesitated at that sally. "Do you claim my education is invalid?"

She shook her head, all flirtation vanished from her face. "No, your grace, only that it might not have been complete."

"You say the most interesting things to me," he said. He wanted to continue the conversation, but the dance set ended and her next partner claimed her, leaving him at a loss.

Was emotion equally as important as knowledge? Or did she say such things only to attract him? He observed how she had not yet sat without a partner. Before the dancing began, she always had two or three men enjoying her laughter and comments.

With him, her flirtation was different. Although they started on the same light footing, somehow the conversation always deepened into something more. He wanted to believe the sentiment was real, but he dared not. He was a duke, and she knew it.

And so she haunted him.

Such as now. He sat at his desk in his library, surrounded by his books—the ideal place for him, the perfect place for study—and he thought about her. On the sheet of paper lying before him, he had begun a poem. An ode to his Lydia-of-the-woods.

Except it was not truly an ode. He did not know how to compose one. Attempting Shakespearean sonnets gave him the same problem. How did one create in iambic pentameter? The lines "with her eyes so blue" did not begin to capture her essence. He tried writing "with her eyes the color of the sky," but those words were no better at portraying the life and laughter that were Lydia.

He crumpled the paper and tossed it aside. Obviously poetry was not his forte. The truth was Lydia was more than a lyrical rendering of her attributes. Yes, she possessed blue eyes, golden curls, and a very kissable mouth, but she was so much more.

Her beauty had attracted him at first; now her ardor and her caring held him in her thrall. He orbited around her as if she was the sun. She was the light in his soul, leading him into the life that pulsed around him. He had lost the desire to hide. He went to dinner parties, took tea, and confronted the British Navy, and it was all due to her influence. Powerful, passionate emotion thrived in Lydia's heart. The strength of the feelings she awoke within him both attracted and frightened him.

She dominated his thoughts, but that was not her fault. His logic told him a fault meant a flaw existed, and there was no flaw in Lydia. She honestly attempted to gain a duke in marriage. It was expected of her—and of every other maiden in the entirety of England. A bachelor duke needed a duchess. He was well aware of her aims.

Should he marry her?

He considered the question, but it was too entangled with his emotions for logic to make headway. Pulling a blank sheet of paper toward him, he drew a line down the middle.

On the left side, he listed what he liked about Lydia. He wrote her beauty down first because that was what he had first noticed. She was certainly talented in her drawing, and he knew from Fanny that her dowry was most respectable.

He put down the externals about Lydia, knowing he overlooked her soul. It was not so easy to list what made Lydia herself. She had a playful side that effortlessly invited him to join in her fairy-tale game. She made him laugh. She believed in him.

But most of all, she listened to him.

With her, he was not the freakish student whom others avoided, nor was he the odd duke whom every woman chased, wanting only his rank. He amended that last thought. Lydia had not made him her prey until she knew his identity. It was those idyllic times at the beginning to which he wished he could return. They had not lasted long, and he regretted that.

After a moment for memory, he turned his attention back to his list. He dipped his pen into the inkwell and prepared to write why Lydia would not make a good duchess.

There was the obvious difference in their stations. She was only of the gentry, but by marrying her, he would lift her to his rank. That obstacle, therefore, was only temporary. As a duke he could do anything he wanted. Ben's release had demonstrated that. His wish was the law. No one could force him to do anything he did not desire.

Even as the relishing of so much power swelled within him, Winterbourne remembered Meg's greeting of Ben. Her shriek of joy still rang in his ears. The way she had clung to Ben left no doubt of her love. The memory of that embrace caused Winterbourne to groan and throw down his pen, spattering ink over the list.

That was what he wanted. To be loved for himself.

Jealousy roared through him. He, the Duke of Winterbourne, envied the head groom at the local inn. Was that not a joke worthy of the gods on Mount Olympus?

Pushing his pen aside, he picked up his list and shook his head. The reason he could not wed Lydia was one he dared not write down. He would always wonder if she loved him or the coronet she could wear. He had reasoned out his answer to whether or not he should marry her, but he did not like the result.

He started to crumple this paper, too, but his glance was caught by the book resting at one corner of his desk. Alexander the Great's biography. He picked it up and skipped the bookmark indicating where he left off, flipping the pages to the end. Alexander had died—whether from poisoning or illness was still debated. When asked "To whom do you leave your kingdom?" he had whispered, "To the strongest," which had led his generals to wars of succession.

Of course, Alexander might have said, "To the best." It all depended upon how one interpreted the meaning of *"Hoti to kratisto."*

For the first time, Winterbourne considered the alternative. Alexander had lived his life by the Homeric motto of Achilles: "Ever to be the best and stand far above the rest." Did Alexander mean to leave his kingdom to the one who was the best? And what did *the best* mean?

The term did not apply to him. According to Cecil's standards, Winterbourne knew he did not measure up as a good duke. Cecil knew far more about the ducal properties, their needs, and their resources. Alexander's kingdom had not outlasted his death. If he died, the dukedom and all its properties would go to Cecil. He would have had no impact on their care. It would be as if he had never existed.

He shuddered at this bleak picture of a wasted life. He did

not want to be a forgotten entity. Alexander had believed personal glory brought immortal renown, and he had sought it by being the forefront on the battlefield. Winterbourne did not face armed enemies, but he possessed a dukedom needing governance. It was past time he took over the reins from Cecil.

He snapped the biography shut and shelved it. He would not need to read the book again. He had learned everything he could from it. Maybe by immersing himself in work, he could finally vanquish Lydia's hold over him. If that was what it took, he would become the best Duke of Winterbourne in his entire lineage.

Winterbourne found Cecil in his office, muttering to himself as he totaled a column of figures. Not wanting to interrupt his secretary's mathematics, Winterbourne took a seat and glanced around. Stacks of periodicals and pamphlets were piled throughout the room. Although the space was cluttered, a sense of order prevailed, as if a system of organization hid behind the papers.

Cecil wrote down a number, looked up, and stood. "Your grace! Forgive me. I did not hear you come in."

Winterbourne waved him back into his seat. "I did not want to distract you. What are you working on?"

His cousin leaned forward, his arm effectively covering his work. "It is nothing important."

He knew Cecil lied, and his curiosity was piqued. "Nothing? It certainly absorbed you so that you did not hear me come in."

"Truly, your grace, you would not be interested."

"Nonsense. Tell me what it is." He smiled at Cecil to coax him, but the firmness in his voice would have been recognized by the harbor master, Mr. Gibson.

Cecil conceded defeat. "I am studying about bringing a canal through this area."

"A canal? Here? Where would you put it?"

"That I am not certain of yet." His cousin riffled through some papers and pulled out a rough map. "I thought it could run from the village of Chelsey because it's on the river."

"Could sufficient water be diverted?"

"I was attempting to calculate the rate of river flow for the past several years when you entered, your grace."

Winterbourne looked at the map and was dubious. "What would be the purpose of this canal?"

"If we build a mill in Chelsey, we can use the canal to ship its goods."

"Why not just build the mill on the river and use its water?"

His cousin drew himself up in indignation. "A canal is not subject to the whims of nature. It has the added benefit of being used for leisure as well as commerce."

"It still must be maintained," Winterbourne said, but he did not want to argue, not when his purpose was to become more involved in his properties. "Shall we ride out and explore the area?"

Cecil's jawbone probably would have hit his desk if his skin had not prevented it. "*You* want to see the site?"

"If you plan to dissect my property, I most certainly do." He stood, ready to throw himself wholeheartedly into his new undertaking. "You must have a place already in mind for this mill. Tell me about it as we ride. What will it produce? What made you select Chelsey?"

The other man eyed him with puzzlement. "I never thought you were interested, your grace."

"I am now. Are you coming?"

Despite the wind-driven weather, they trekked to Chelsey.

Winterbourne listened carefully to Cecil's explanations. He asked questions, but the answers made him more dubious about a mill and a canal. He kept his doubts to himself, determined to study the prospect further. By concentrating on the issue, perhaps he could override Lydia's memory.

For the next two weeks, he hounded Cecil's steps. They rode over the Home Farm, and he met with his tenants. Despite their minor complaints, he could see that Cecil had managed the properties fairly, and he learned of the vast resources that made up the Winterbourne dukedom. There was more to it than just the lands in Essex.

The work prevented him from participating in the social round. If Lydia called for tea, she shared it with Fanny. He was not at home. In the evening, after a full day of riding, he preferred to retire with the books on crop rotation and the pamphlets on the textile industry. Although there were no official texts like *The Iliad*, he was a student again. Enthusiasm filled him. This was something he could understand.

He enjoyed the feeling, but always he was aware that there was one direction in which he never rode—toward the clearing in the woods. He might not see Lydia, but he continued to encounter her in his memory. When the words blurred on the pages or the hoofbeats on the road faded away into dreaming, he lost himself in remembering her. Fighting it was a losing battle, and at last he surrendered. He would have to meet her again—privately.

Cecil and he were getting ready for another ride to scout out the river when Fanny entered.

"Are you going out again?" she asked with a pout forming on her face.

"Yes," Winterbourne said. He did not tell her that this final visit would determine if engineers and surveyors were needed.

"You are never here when callers come."

"I regret the absence." He shrugged into the coat the butler held.

"On the days you state you will be at home to callers, you should be at home," Fanny pointed out.

"You are here." He did not want to waste his time with chattering visitors. He had no time. More and more he was discovering how much there was to his dukedom.

"Yes, I am always here," she muttered.

Winterbourne ignored her. Instead, he beckoned a footman aside and handed him the note he had dashed off moments ago. He had made his decision. "See that this is delivered to Meg, the ladies' maid at Grenville Manor."

"What is that?" Cecil asked as he shrugged into the winter coat the butler held for him.

"Just a note I want delivered," Winterbourne said.

He caught Fanny staring at him and quelled her gaze with a haughtily raised eyebrow. She turned away, and he breathed an inward sigh of relief.

He had sealed it so no one could read the word *Sketching?* on the paper. It was not signed. Although it was sent to Meg, he was certain it would end up in Lydia's hands when the maid puzzled over the note's meaning. Lydia would know from whom it came. He must see her again. Even work did not banish her spell. Tomorrow he would go to the clearing in the woods. What he hoped to achieve by meeting her alone, he did not know. He knew only that he must see her again. For one day, he would leave Cecil to his own devices.

Together they mounted up and trotted along the now familiar route past the village of Chelsey. At the proposed mill site, they tramped through the dried reeds, muddying their boots in the process. A light breeze blew from the river. The damp air added to the chill trying to gnaw through his wool coat. The gray day did not make the place appear more inviting.

At last Winterbourne shook his head. "I am sorry, Cecil. It will not work."

With his hands on hips, Cecil turned from surveying the bank. He blinked away the dreamy expression on his face. "What did you say, your grace?"

"The canal. I see no need for it. The river appears sufficiently large and deep for shipping." To mitigate the blow, he added, "A mill might still work here."

"No canal?"

"The mill is a fine idea. I have been reading about the possibilities. I'll concede the mill might work and allow you to hire some engineers to inspect the site."

"Canals are the way of the future."

"Building a dock here would be far less expensive." Winterbourne tried to make his voice conciliatory. The project meant so much to his cousin.

"I wanted a canal," Cecil said in a small voice.

"Investigate the mill prospects first," Winterbourne said firmly.

"Yes, your grace." For a moment, his cousin looked lost, and then his face brightened. "A canal should be built in the springtime anyways. I will begin it while you are in Greece."

"I will not be going."

There was no need to go to Greece. The distance he could put between Lydia and himself did not matter. These past two weeks had proven a trip would provide no surcease from her memory. There was no escape. He might as well stay and be the best duke he could be right here.

"You're not?"

The disappointed shock on Cecil's face sent a spike of doubt through Winterbourne. Had his neglect of his duties given Cecil ideas above his position? With a shiver, he shook off the question and said, "You have shown me quite a bit about the estate. I am assuming my responsibilities. It will no longer all be on your shoulders."

Cecil protested, "But I know what should be done."

"I will rely on your advice, but I will make the decisions." He turned and headed back to the horses.

"I wanted a canal," Cecil muttered.

Winterbourne ignored the complaint and mounted up. He was the one now setting the course of the dukedom. If only he could be so decisive when it came to dealing with Lydia.

Chapter Eleven

L ydia almost did not go to the forest clearing. Yesterday, Meg, with a great number of smirks and exaggerated sly gestures, had delivered the note from the duke. Despite Meg's hovering interest, Lydia did not enlighten her as to the meaning of the note's contents. She knew what he meant by that single word *Sketching?* It had weighed upon her mind even as she joined her mother for a round of calls. Should she go to the woods?

Even as she dressed the next morning, she had not resolved the issue. The autumn weather possessed a definite chill. She selected her blue woolen dress with the black embroidery tracing the neckline. Although it was a more severe style than she usually wore, Lydia liked it. She felt pretty while wearing it, even if her coat would hide the trim from view. She would know it was there. That knowledge would increase her poise, and she was going to need every bit of confidence available to her this morning.

Lydia paused before the looking glass to adjust her skirt. She had just made her decision. If she needed confidence this morning, then she must be expecting to face Winterbourne. With a lift of her chin, she straightened her shoulders. She *would* meet him.

With a skill born of practice, Lydia slipped out of the manor without her mother's notice and was the first to arrive at the clearing. The overcast sky refused to succumb to the sun's rays, which were bravely attempting to burn away the gray. The leaves had lost their golds and reds. The few remaining on the branches hung as limp as wet dishrags, their autumn glory dull and past. Dampness clung to the air, bringing to mind both past and future rains.

She kicked at the pile of leaves beneath her feet. Although she carried her sketching supplies, she did not have her blanket. She had misplaced it somewhere. Its loss mattered little. Sketching was only a ruse. Curiosity ate at Lydia. Why had he sent that note? What did he expect to say once they met?

Last time, she had hoped to melt that barrier between them with the payment of her kiss. For a moment she had believed she had succeeded, but he had gone away without making an offer.

What was the purpose of this meeting?

Lydia had not waited very long when she saw him hurrying toward her and heard the leaves crunching beneath his boots. Despite her resolve to treat him with perfect manners, pleasure bubbled within her.

As always, he presented a fine figure of a man. His heavy brown coat could not disguise his slim build. His breeches were tan and his boots polished. His hat sat at a rakish angle atop his head. She doubted he meant the effect. He strode so quickly that his walking stick was clutched in his hand like a club instead of languidly swaying from side to side.

"You came," he greeted her.

She could not mistake the gladness on his face, and her heart skipped a beat. "With such a mysterious note, how could I resist?"

"I did not know how else to contact you."

He reached out to grasp her hands, but she already held her sketching supplies. After an instant of amused fumbling, she laid one hand in his. His grasp was warm and strong. A tingle shivered from her head to her toes. She wanted to nestle close to him, but her mother's advice to be reserved held her back.

"Why did you want to meet me here?" she asked. "We've seen each other elsewhere. Why here?"

"You are always surrounded by men. I cannot talk with you then."

Delight sputtered within her. He *had* noticed her flirtations, just as her mother predicted.

"We are the only ones here," she said with a significant glance around. Only trees surrounded the two of them, their trunks wide and tall.

"Yes, we are."

He looked deep into her eyes as if he searched them for something. She stayed still under his scrutiny, gazing back. Beneath his initial gladness, distress lined his face.

Something drove him. Something she did not understand. "What is it?" she asked, concern lacing her voice. "Is there anything wrong?"

He dropped her hand and turned away. He took a couple of steps and stopped. Mastering himself, he drew a deep breath and faced her. "Lydia—Miss Grenville—I don't know how to say this, but I must ask you—" He broke off, his courage apparently once again shaken.

A slight gasp escaped her lips. Wonder crept into her heart, along with doubt. Such words usually preceded an offer. Did she dare to hope? "I am listening," she said softly.

A faint smile ghosted across his lips. "Yes, you do listen to me. You always have—even before you knew who I was." He straightened his shoulders. "I do not find it easy to talk about this. About emotion. I am much more at home among my Greeks and my studies."

He paused.

Believing she must say something, Lydia said, "I never knew there was so much history about the Greeks."

His smile became more pronounced. "Always you are willing to follow my conversational lead. Why, I wonder, is that? Because I am a duke?"

"A duke? Why does that matter?"

The loud report of a gun sounded. A bullet slammed into the tree trunk behind him. An unseen bird squawked and flapped its wings in flight. Winterbourne's head whipped around to see pieces of bark flying from the shot's impact. In the next instant, he launched himself on top of Lydia, crashing her to the ground. Gasping for air, she looked up and saw his face only inches from hers. His eyes were round with fright, and his breath brushed her cheek. It was an oddly reassuring touch.

"What was that?" she asked.

"Someone is shooting."

"At us?" Her voice rose in panic.

"Are you hurt?"

"Shooting at us? Why would anyone do that?"

"I'm certain it was an accident. Are you hurt? Nothing hit you, did it?" His hands moved over her shoulders, searching for a wound.

Suddenly aware of their position with her beneath the length of him, Lydia stilled under his touch. "No, no, I'm fine," she said, breathless.

His gaze fell away from hers in awkwardness. He pushed himself up on his arms, still over her yet no longer touching her. She shivered, either in fear or in the sudden chill from the loss of his warmth.

Glancing around the empty clearing, he called out, "You didn't hit us. We're all right. You can come out now."

He looked in the direction of the shot. Nothing stirred. Even the breeze was motionless, as if waiting.

In the silence a sense of danger grew within Lydia, and she whispered, "Is anyone there?"

Winterbourne called again. "Don't be frightened. You can come out."

The quiet remained. Lydia's heart beat so hard the blood rushed in her ears like a swift-flowing river. "Maybe he left."

Cautiously, Winterbourne got to his feet and, with measured steps, approached the area. Sitting up, Lydia watched him search. Her hands trembled, and she clasped them together, squeezing them in an effort to provide reassurance.

He peered around several of the trees and kicked at the gray underbrush. The breeze suddenly sighed through the branches, but nothing else moved.

Coming back to her, he said, "No one is there. He must have run away when he realized he had nearly shot us."

Lydia took the hand he held out and rose. She did not release his grip, and his other hand now covered one of hers, making her feel secure in his grasp. Her heart should be slowing from her fear, but it continued to race.

"Why do you think he shot at you?" she asked.

"I doubt it was deliberate. Probably an accident."

"An accident?"

He shrugged. "Likely a poacher who mistook me for a deer."

"You look nothing like a deer," she said. "Besides, why didn't he come forward once you called to him?"

"Fear, I should think. The punishment for poaching is severe."

Lydia wanted to believe his assurances. "Or maybe he ran because he missed you."

"Missed *me*?" Amazement wreathed his face.

"What if he *was* shooting at you?"

"Nonsense. Why would anyone want to shoot me?"

"You're the duke." The more she thought about it, the more frightened Lydia became. Her grip on his hands tightened. "Oh, you must be careful!"

"Lydia, I appreciate your concern, but no one wants to shoot me. I do not have an enemy in the world."

"Dukes always have enemies," she said, warning him.

"Not this one," he said lightly. "Why would anyone be against me? Before I was a duke, I was a student of ancient Greece. Do you truly think that scholars go around the countryside shooting at other scholars?"

She shook her head. "You're a duke now, not a student."

"Lydia, the shot was surely just an accident. I have done nothing as a duke to make anyone that angry."

Gazing into his face, she knew he would not believe her. "I hope not."

Maybe he was correct. Maybe the shot was accidental. She wanted to believe that. She wanted him to be safe—for her—because she loved him.

The realization stunned her even as she acknowledged its truth. She loved him. Not because he was a duke, but for the man he was. A man who could join her silly play about a fairy princess. A man who respected her thoughts, even if he did not agree with them. A man who sent fire racing through her veins with only his touch. When he had knocked her to the ground just now, not all of her breathlessness had been due to the impact. Even as he continued to hold her hands, she could feel his strength and concern moving up her arms until her entire body was embraced by him.

She glanced away from his gaze and around the clearing. It remained the same dismal site it had been before, with its damp leaves and gray overcast. Yet now two emotions battled within her. Love and fear. They both centered around the same man.

"We should not stay here," she said.

"The poacher is long gone."

"I want to go home." When he offered her his arm, she took it. "You will be careful."

"Because you ask it, I will be."

Alert, they headed through the woods toward Grenville Manor. Lydia's gaze continued to search for any whisper of movement indicating the presence of a threat. Once she cast a quick look backwards.

"He is not there," Winterbourne said.

She saw nothing. "You are correct." Taking a few more steps, she said, "Maybe we should not meet here any longer. With winter coming, the poachers will be more active."

His brows drew down. "You would let an accident destroy the fairy kingdom?"

Yes, her heart cried. *I would do anything to protect you.* Aloud, she said, "With the weather turning bad, I cannot continue to use sketching as an excuse to slip away."

"Can you not think of another reason?"

"No." They had reached the edge of the woods. It was time to say farewell.

He frowned. "Spring is a long ways off."

"We will meet at the county's functions," she reminded him.

"Yes, we will."

He bent forward. Was he going to kiss her? He lifted her hand resting on his arm and pressed it to his lips. The tender gesture sent her heart pounding again, spreading warmth throughout her body.

With an effort, she said, "I will go on from here alone."

"I should walk you safely to your door."

"No, we should not be seen. Besides, you should take the road back to the castle as quickly as possible."

Her request didn't fool him. "And it is safer than going through the woods?"

"Yes." She could not lie about something so important.

"I feel the same way about you. I will watch you from here."

"Very well." Lydia needed no second speech. She scurried across the lawn, her sketching supplies clutched tightly to her breast. At the door, she looked back and saw his wave before he plunged back behind the screen of trees, going through the woods instead of along the road.

"Be careful, my love," she prayed.

At that moment, she realized she had never discovered what he meant to tell her. He had mentioned emotion was difficult for him. He truly was more at home among his Greeks, but something had driven him out of the past. Something strong. Passion perhaps?

She hugged the possibility to herself to savor. He was a duke, but that was not why she wanted him. She wanted him for himself.

Fanny leaned against the tree, hidden from view. She blinked, wondering if her eyes played tricks upon her. Had she truly spotted Winterbourne—with Lydia? At a secret meeting? Unchaperoned?

She rubbed her hands against the bark, its roughness helping to steady the disbelief tumbling through her mind. She had to be certain. She had to risk another look.

Inhaling a lungful of air as if she feared the couple would overhear her breathing, Fanny peeked around the tree's trunk. She was not close enough to hear what they said, but her eyes had not lied.

Winterbourne stood next to Lydia.

They held hands. He looked deep into her eyes and she gazed back. Would they kiss?

Fanny's plan to follow Winterbourne had yielded far more surprising fruit than she'd anticipated. Despite his protests, she had wondered if there was something between the duke and Lydia. The note had flamed her suspicions from smoldering embers to ignited kindling. Today, she knew, he did not plan to traverse the estate with Cecil.

When she saw Winterbourne stealing away from the castle in such a furtive manner, she had determined to follow. By the time she had put on her coat, bonnet, and gloves, and left the castle, she just caught a glimpse of him disappearing into the woods. Determined not to lose him, she had scampered across the wide lawn.

When she reached the trees, she pressed a hand to her breast, gasping for breath. He moved so easily with his boots and breeches, while her skirt hampered her legs and her soft shoes skidded on the damp ground. The wet seeped into her shoes, making her grimace. She would have returned home, except she spotted him disappearing over the top of the hill. Having already ruined her shoes, she refused to turn back in defeat.

She struggled up the slope and at last reached the top. Gasping some more, she looked around at the barren trees, the fallen piles of soggy leaves, and the gray underbrush.

There was no sign of which way Winterbourne had gone.

Her shoulders sagged with disappointment. The thrill of a secret being discovered had provided the energy to her body, giving her the impetus to force herself up the hill. With nothing to reward her efforts, she wandered amidst the trees on the chance that something might grab her attention. Even the woods ended up being filled with boredom.

Giving up, she started back toward the castle. A shot sounded and she jumped. She glanced around with caution. It had been close but not next to her.

Should she go home? It would be the sensible thing to do with a hunter in the woods. Her boredom vanished. Something both thrilling and dangerous was occurring. Keeping a wary eye out for the hunter, she headed in the direction of the shot. She heard voices but could not distinguish the words, and excitement built within her.

Then, peering around a tree, she saw a sight that rewarded all her efforts. Winterbourne and Lydia alone in the woods.

"O-o-oh!" Fanny breathed. Her eyes widened with delight. "The scandal!"

Chapter Twelve

$\mathcal{F}$or three days, Lydia waited on pins and needles in fear of hearing the duke had been killed. Yet no such news flashed through the neighborhood. Indeed, there had been no callers to Grenville Manor, so Lydia and her mother, in search of congenial company, climbed the steps of the Fisher residence to pay a call and take tea. Built in the early Georgian style, the house showed distinct inspiration from Greek architecture, with four soaring columns framing the entranceway and an equal number of windows on either side.

Tucking her hands into her muff, Lydia reflected that Winterbourne had introduced her to many things. The warm glow spreading through her at thoughts of him had nothing to do with the coat or hat she wore. It radiated from the amazing knowledge that she loved him. He was a man out of her usual ken. Not because he was a duke, but because he was a man who respected her intelligence and solicited her opinions.

The Fishers' butler did not immediately open the front door upon their arrival. He should have heard the carriage pull up. The existence of two other carriages in front proved they were not the first visitors.

Her mother knocked. Surprisingly, the door did not instantly swing open, but after a pause the butler did open it. He stood solidly in the crack between the door and the frame.

Her mother started forward. "Good afternoon," she said.

The butler blocked her path and did not open the door wider. "Mrs. Fisher is not at home."

"Not at home?" her mother echoed.

Lydia's gaze swung to the carriages parked on the drive behind them. One of the horses shook his mane and stamped his foot.

"Of course Mary is at home," she said.

He stared at a point somewhere between the two of them. "I was instructed to say neither Mrs. Fisher nor Miss Mary is at home to you."

"To us? Why not?"

"It is not my place to speculate."

"I would like to see Mary." Lydia made as if to push past him.

Her mother's hand on her arm restrained her. "No, Lydia. If they do not wish to see us, we should not force our presence upon them."

The butler's stare never wavered.

To him, her mother said, "Tell Mrs. Fisher that we regret calling at such an inconvenient moment and shall return at another time."

With her hand gripping Lydia's elbow, her mother guided her down the steps. With the groom's assistance, they climbed back into their carriage and set off on the return home.

"I do not understand," Lydia said as she adjusted her skirt's folds. "Why would the Fishers refuse to see us?"

"It is very rude behavior. I am certain they did not mean it."

"Perhaps their butler misunderstood his instructions," Lydia offered hopefully.

"Perhaps. I don't know."

"Mrs. Fisher will wonder why we did not call today. You should write a note explaining what happened."

Her mother plucked at her coat. "That would be the correct thing to do, but how do I address how rude her servant has been?"

"Write that we were denied admittance. Let her find out the reason."

"You may be right. I just hate it whenever these upsets occur in society. The time spent on them is most unpleasant." Her mother leaned her head against the back of the seat and closed her eyes.

In the shadowed light of the carriage, Lydia could see how much the incident had distressed her mother. Lines etched furrows from her nose to her mouth, and the skin under her eyes had the slightest sag, emphasized by the play of the gray light.

Her mother asked, "You have not heard any rumors about us, have you, Lydia?"

"Rumors? Of course not. What has someone been saying?"

Lifting her hand to her forehead, her mother said, "I haven't heard any, either. I'm trying to understand why we were treated so rudely."

For the first time, a frisson of alarm shivered within Lydia. Had her secret meetings with Winterbourne been discovered? The scandal would break her parents' hearts and destroy her reputation. Hidden inside the muff, her fingers twisted in agitation.

Nonsense, she reassured herself.

She had nothing to worry about. They had been very careful. No one knew that they'd met.

Then she remembered that shot. Someone else knew.

Lydia was dressing for dinner when her father's shout roared through the manor, causing the windows to tremble in their frames.

"Lydia!" he bellowed. "Lydia!"

Her eyes met Meg's in the looking glass. The maid's hands stilled in Lydia's hair with the hairbrush upraised. Alarm exploded in Lydia. Her father never shouted at her. He cosseted her. Something must be seriously wrong.

"That's enough for now," Lydia said to Meg. She pushed back her chair and rose. "I must go to my father immediately."

The maid's eyes widened until they were the size of buckets. "Oh, miss, I've never heard him yell so."

"Lydia!" he roared again.

With such a command, she had no expectation of waiting for a servant to summon her to him. His voice demanded immediate obedience. She swallowed the lump in her throat and discovered her palms were already damp. She pressed them against her skirt and went downstairs.

Her father stood in the center of the drawing room, his hands on his hips and a scowl smearing his face. With the angry brows and narrowed eyes, he did not look at all like her usual papa, the one whom she could twist around her finger. Fear grew within her as she stepped across the threshold.

"What is it, Papa?"

He glowered at her. "Is it true? Is this tale your mother brings the truth?"

"What tale is that, Papa?" Her voice quavered as she tried to ward off the inevitable.

"She said you've been seeing Winterbourne alone and in the woods!"

She glanced at her mother, who lay collapsed on a chair, her face splotched with tears. Lydia's insides twisted like a tangled skein of yarn. "Who told you?"

"The vicar's wife." Her mother sniffed. "I thought of visiting her once we returned home. She's a good Christian woman. She wouldn't turn me away if I called." Her fingers pulled at her handkerchief, tearing it. "Mrs. Pennyfeather could not even look me in the eye when she told me."

"Well, Lydia?" her father demanded.

Lydia took a deep breath, already feeling her tears beginning to brim. "Yes, Papa, I did meet him in the woods, but honestly, nothing happened."

"Oh!" her mother wailed. "That my daughter could act in such a fashion!"

Lydia ran to kneel at her side. "Nothing happened, Mother. I swear it."

Her mother did not even bother wiping away the tears pouring down her face. "You are ruined. Ruined! The story is everywhere. It cannot be hushed up."

. "How could you behave so?" her father demanded, his bellow broken.

Through her tears, Lydia could see the sorrow and the shame engraved upon their faces. Her father's normally upright posture slouched as if a heavy burden weighed him down, and all of her mother's beauty was dissolved by the salt of her tears. For the first time, Lydia realized that the consequences of her actions affected them, too. She did not act alone.

"I'm sorry," she said, tears breaking her voice. "We didn't do anything wrong."

"It doesn't matter," her mother said. "You're ruined anyway. You will be fortunate to marry a farmer or a merchant after this scandal. How could you do such a thing?"

"I didn't mean to meet him," Lydia tried to explain. "It happened by accident. I was sketching, and he came by."

"Where was Meg?" Her father started for the door. "She should be dismissed for leaving you alone."

Lydia sprang to her feet. "Wait! It was not her fault. I slipped away from her, too. Meg didn't know."

"A deceiving, deceptive daughter!" he exclaimed.

"I'm sorry, Papa. I didn't think. I didn't even know who he was at first."

His jaw dropped. "Didn't know? You met him unchaperoned, and you didn't know who he was?"

She wrung her hands. "I thought he was the duke's secretary."

"A secretary!" her mother wailed. "You ruined yourself for someone you thought was a secretary?"

"I found out later he was Winterbourne," Lydia said miserably in an attempt to make amends.

"This is not finished," her father declared. "Duke or no, he is going to do right by my daughter." He stalked toward the door.

Her mother put her hand to her mouth. "Josiah, what do you mean to do?"

"He is going to marry my daughter. No man trifles with my daughter's reputation and walks away. Not my daughter!"

"Papa, you can't!"

"I can't? Why not?"

"Nothing happened between us. You can't force a marriage on nothing."

"Nothing, eh?" He glared at Lydia. "When did you first meet?"

"The end of September. It was all quite innocent. I showed him a drawing I'd done of the castle."

He nodded. "Since September. You claim it was all so innocent, yet you met more than once."

"It was innocent!"

"Indeed. In all that time, over a month, not once did either of you behave inappropriately? You discussed art as if you were in a drawing room. There was never any attempt at a small liberty? Never any attempt at perhaps a small kiss?"

He stared at her. Lydia could not meet his eyes. She started to protest because she knew she must. No matter what Winterbourne's kisses meant to her, she could not expose their existence.

"Papa—"

He cut her off. "It wasn't so innocent, was it?"

It hurt to breathe. Between the sobs struggling to escape her throat and the protests she must speak, a lump blocked them. Her lungs ached.

She tried. "Papa, he was a gentleman always. We talked about Greece and my drawing."

"Pretty words have lured many a maiden into ruin—you included. You have behaved terribly."

Unable to argue any longer, she gazed down at the carpet beneath her feet. Her father was right. She had behaved terribly. Her tears blurred the Oriental rug's pattern into a smudge of blues, golds, and reds.

After a moment, her father declared, "You will be a duchess, after all, but I am ashamed of the method by which you won your new rank."

She heard him leave the room. His footfalls dragged even as they moved forward with determination. He was on his way to do his duty. Her mother's sniffs alternated with her sobs. Lydia did not move from her spot on the rug.

What could she say? There were no words to halt her father's mission. There were no words to soothe her mother's heartbreak. There were no words to erase her meetings with Winterbourne.

She would marry the duke. Despite her actions, it seemed she had achieved her desire. She would be a duchess—and wed the man she loved. It appeared that she was victorious, but Lydia knew she had failed.

He would not like being forced into marriage, and that resentment would grow. Every morning at breakfast, every evening at dinner, whenever he saw her, he would be reminded that he had not chosen her as his wife. Eventually, she would avoid him. Slowly her love would die from lack of affection between them.

She had not succeeded in a brilliant betrothal during her London Season, but this was the greater failure. She had lost her chance for love.

Because Winterbourne had refused the canal idea, he thought he should listen to Cecil's interminable reports with at least a pretense of attention. However, he could not prevent his eyes from straying to the clock resting on the mantel of the library's fireplace. It was not ticking nearly fast enough until dinner should be announced.

Cecil droned on. "Mr. Sutton sent a request for his roof to be repaired. I researched the records on his tenancy. He often complains, but it would be wise if the roof were inspected. Something like that should not be allowed to degrade when a small bit of maintenance could prevent further expense later. Would the day after tomorrow suit your grace to confer with the man?"

Winterbourne waved a hand in acquiescence. By all rights, such a task belonged to Cecil. After all, he was the one who oversaw such matters, but Winterbourne had wanted to lose himself in the minutiae of work. He could not now complain when the details wearied him.

"I checked through the ledgers, and it appears that money for a contractor—" Cecil's voice halted, checked by a commotion in the hall.

The door opened, framing the butler. "Mr. Josiah Grenville to see you, your grace."

He had no time to present the tray where a white calling card lay. Before Winterbourne could even respond if he was at home or not, the stout man elbowed his way past the servant.

"Winterbourne!"

Lydia's father! With trepidation, he rose to his feet. "What is the trouble, sir?"

"You, your grace, are the trouble." Mr. Grenville thrust his hands on his hips. From beneath his bushy brows, his eyes narrowed as they glared at him.

"I am?" With sudden clarity, Winterbourne knew why Josiah was here. "I think we should discuss this matter privately."

"I'm not leaving."

Winterbourne looked at Cecil.

Pursing his lips, Cecil shuffled his papers into a stack. Maximizing his inconvenience, he stood. "If we can discuss these matters at a later time, your grace?"

"Yes, yes." Winterbourne ushered him to the door and closed it firmly behind him. He turned back to his belligerent guest. "What is this about?"

"You know," Josiah said. "You've compromised my daughter, Lydia."

He did not try to protest. Such words would only be useless and lies. He would not lie. "Our meetings were friendly—nothing more."

"She said you kissed her."

"Innocent kisses only." Despite the night cool permeating the room, Winterbourne felt sweat dampen his skin.

"Meeting my daughter—in the woods—alone—unchaperoned—is not innocent." He drew himself up to his full height, making himself level with Winterbourne's gaze. "You, your grace, are a despoiler of a young maiden."

"Now wait a minute!"

Josiah would not be stopped. "You have ruined her reputation. The scandal is widespread."

"What scandal?"

"My daughter is compromised. It is your fault. I am here to see you redeem her virtue."

"But nothing happened between us," Winterbourne protested in desperation.

"She made the same claim," Josiah said. He did not take his eyes off Winterbourne. "Perhaps it is true, but it doesn't matter. You must marry Lydia immediately."

Winterbourne's apprehension disappeared in astonished shock. "Marry Lydia?"

"She was a good girl of genteel family. Surely you did not expect to use my daughter and toss her aside?"

"I did not use her at all."

Josiah continued inexorably. "I expect the banns to be read the first time on Sunday. The marriage will be in three weeks."

Goaded beyond endurance, Winterbourne snapped, "I will not marry her."

Josiah's face turned white. His mouth opened and closed several times before he managed to speak. "What did you say?"

"I am not marrying Lydia. We did nothing wrong. Therefore, I refuse to be punished." He regretted his previous outburst. Obviously he should have rephrased his stark refusal so as not to incite Josiah into rash speech.

"You met her alone."

"I apologize for that." Winterbourne felt very aloof and very cold, as if he were far away in a high, dark tower. His unruly emotions had already trapped him once in this meeting into speaking before he thought.

"It will take more than your apology to repair Lydia's reputation," Josiah said.

"Since nothing happened, her reputation will remain intact."

"There is scandal attached to her name." A note of pleading crept into Josiah's voice. "You can't mean to treat my girl this way."

Winterbourne had not been so lost in his studies at university that he did not know how strongly ladies sought to keep scandal from their names. Yet Josiah's demand had appeared so suddenly and so abruptly that he had responded in a fit of frustration.

He drew a deep breath. "I am certain you exaggerate the gossip."

"I do not. Please, your grace, you must marry my daughter."

"I assure you, nothing occurred which demands such a solution." The other man looked so woebegone that Winterbourne tried be conciliatory. "In a short time, the gossip will fasten on some other overblown story."

Josiah shook his head. "My daughter will still be ruined, and it is your fault." He took two steps forward until he was directly in front of Winterbourne. "You force me into this, your grace. Name your seconds."

"My seconds?" Winterbourne stared. "What for?"

"I will meet you on the court of honor to redeem Lydia's name."

Winterbourne should have laughed at the absurdity of the request. The prospect of a duel was truly comical—that he would fight with a man at least thirty years his senior. He knew Josiah hunted, but a hunting gun and a dueling pistol were two different types of firearms. Winterbourne had never participated in a duel, but he knew that much. Besides, what if someone got hurt or even killed? Dueling was not something to be indulged in for sport. How could he ever face Lydia again—if he killed her father?

"No," he said. "I won't duel with you."

Desperation filled Josiah. "You must."

"No."

Josiah lifted his hand and struck Winterbourne's cheek. He staggered under the blow's force.

"Now you must meet me," Josiah said with satisfaction.

Even though he could feel his skin reddening from the blow's sting, he would not fight Lydia's father. He crossed his arms. "I refuse."

Josiah stared at him and then his shoulders sagged. He turned away and started slowly for the door. "Lydia," he said. "My poor girl."

Winterbourne watched him go, pity in his heart. The man obviously loved his daughter, but he was foolish to think that their innocent meetings required marriage.

Because he was a duke, *everyone* demanded from him and expected him to fulfill their desires. The constant claims wore on him, and he had no place of refuge, of sanctuary, remaining. The library was crowded with Lydia's memory, Cecil's reports, and now Josiah Grenville's ultimatum. He had nowhere left to retreat, except into his rank.

He was the Duke of Winterbourne. He would make his own decisions—without bending to the wishes of others. He had his own will, and one thing he would do without anyone else commanding him. Rubbing his cheek, he vowed he would choose his own wife, when he wished to marry, thank you very much.

Chapter Thirteen

*L*ydia sat on the couch beside her mother. Neither of them moved or spoke as they suffered together through the long wait for Mr. Grenville's return. Sometimes her mother sniffed. Occasionally Lydia wiped her eyes with her handkerchief. After some time had passed, Lydia's hand crept toward her mother's lap. Her mother put her hand over Lydia's, and they gripped each other tightly, seeking solace. The waiting was the hardest part.

The sun had long since set, and darkness shrouded the drawing room. Only the flickering of the flames in the hearth illuminated the room.

What answer, Lydia wondered, would her father bring back from Winterbourne?

She had wanted to be a duchess. Since she could remember, high rank in her marriage had been her whole goal in life. The scandal would force Winterbourne to offer for her. She would succeed and become the Duchess of Winterbourne, but this was not how she'd wanted it to happen.

Her secret hope had been a marriage based on love, although she would have accepted one begun on affection. Now she wasn't likely to have even that much. How could he care for her when their marriage was forced by scandal?

Yes, he had participated in the scandalous meetings, too, but they were both to blame. She'd known it was wrong and had continued to play the fairy princess. One did not treat society's strictures lightly. She knew that now, even as she wished such rules did not bind her. She had liked playacting, but she had yearned for his kisses.

Despite the rampant speculation, Lydia doubted anyone had actually seen them. The speculation was enough to fuel the clacking tongues—and it was enough to coerce a duke into marriage.

The door opened, and Lydia looked up with a start, expecting to see her father, but it was only the butler carrying two candles, which he set on the table. Then he withdrew, shutting the door behind him. The candles fought against the shrouded darkness of night, but Lydia was too miserable to be heartened by such a small sign of brightness.

At length, she heard the carriage crunch the gravel drive outside the window. She squeezed her mother's hand hard, suddenly fearful. Her heart pounded and her hearing concentrated on her father, seeking to discover a hint to her fate before he could tell her.

Her father's steps sounded slow and heavy on the other side of the door. They halted for a moment. The blood rushed to Lydia's head, making her feel faint. What answer did Winterbourne send? Her father had returned alone. What fate did that portend?

The door opened and he came into the room. His shoulders were slumped, his head bowed, and his arms hung loosely at his sides. He carried a burden of disgrace, one she had piled upon him.

Lydia released her mother's hand and slowly rose. "Papa?"

He looked at her with such despair in his eyes that she

clutched her hands to her breast as if to steady the sudden lurch of her heart. "Papa, what is it? What did he say?"

Her father shook his head. "I couldn't make him do it. I couldn't make him marry you."

His words seemed to come from a long way off. The faintness she had felt before now threatened to overwhelm her senses. "He won't marry me?"

"He refused?" Her mother shuddered to her feet and threw herself into her husband's arms. "He won't marry her?"

"I failed," he said. "He does not care that our daughter is ruined."

"Ruined," her mother whispered and then she wailed, "Ruined!"

Lydia flinched. The word struck her like a rock thrown by mean village boys at the old women they disliked, women who were outcasts from society. Now she was a pariah, no longer welcome in the company of decent people. She could expect the ladies to draw their skirts aside at her approach. Would the boys also throw rocks at her?

"What did he say?" Lydia asked with every bit of steadiness in her voice she could muster. She must be brave.

"He admitted to the meetings and, like you, claimed they were innocent, but he didn't seem to understand how serious they were. He thought the scandal would die down. It was as though the gossip would not besmirch you—or him." Her father pulled her mother close and repeated in a lost voice, "He didn't seem to understand."

Her father was right. "No," Lydia said. "He wouldn't understand. He is a scholar so lost in his studies of the past, he cannot grasp how society functions today." She smiled without humor. "He never did fit in—either as a student or as a duke. Society's dictates always remained a mystery to him."

She stepped toward her parents. "I am truly sorry for this

scandal. I know I have greatly disappointed you. When you can, please forgive me."

The despair overshadowing them made her heart ache for them. No matter how much they loved her, she had failed in fulfilling their picture of a perfect daughter. Regret swelled within her. She patted her mother's shoulder.

"I am sorry," she said again before turning away.

At a deliberate pace, she left the drawing room and walked to the stairs. In the shadowed recesses of the hall, she glimpsed the clustered servants. The butler, the cook, the maids—all of them were affected by the disgrace she'd brought upon the household. No longer could they hold up their heads among their peers.

"I apologize," she whispered to them.

There was no response. Maybe they did not hear her. Or maybe an outcast was invisible to the servants as well. She climbed the steps to her room.

Meg waited there. The red-rimmed eyes testified to the other girl's tears. Mutely, she began to help Lydia prepare for bed.

Lydia was grateful for her silence. She didn't want another word spoken in her presence. Words hurt. They said no. They rejected you.

Meg sniffed.

Lydia held up her hand in protest. "Don't say it."

Kneeling to pull off Lydia's stockings, Meg ignored her request. "Oh, miss, I'm sorry for you. It's just terrible. Terrible. You don't deserve this scandal."

Lydia refused to hide behind false innocence. "Maybe I do. I did meet him, after all."

"And why shouldn't you? He's a good man. What woman wouldn't want to meet him?"

In spite of herself, a ray of humor lightened Lydia's spirits at how quickly Meg switched her defense. The maid was loyal, and that trait provided a bit of soothing balm for her broken heart. "You are right. I couldn't resist meeting him."

Meg stood and smoothed the stockings in her hand. "Of course not. A good man and a duke—why, no lady could resist such a combination."

Lydia gave a rueful laugh of acknowledgment.

"Do you love him?" the maid asked.

"Meg! That is too bold."

She was not cowed. "I know love, miss. I love my Ben. I couldn't be without him. Is it that way for you, too?"

Lydia's thoughts swirled. She had loved Winterbourne, and he had rejected her. Did she still love him? Did her heart still yearn for him? Did she still long to touch him, to laugh with him, to share her thoughts with him?

"Yes," she whispered. "I do love him."

Meg gently laid her hands on Lydia's shoulders. "Then I pray you can be together the way Ben and I are."

"You are very kind," Lydia said, overwhelmed.

"I would do anything for you—and for him," Meg said.

After Meg had blown out the candle and departed, Lydia lay in her bed staring up at the darkness. Her eyes itched from her tears, but no more remained to flow. She was beyond crying for herself.

Instead, she considered what Meg had made her acknowledge. She still loved Winterbourne. As she had told her father, he didn't understand how society behaved. His milieu was the world of the mind. She had grown up knowing society's rules, yet in his presence she had allowed her emotions full play. To prevent the rules from being lightly broken, society imposed severe consequences.

She faced them now, not gladly but with courage. She would continue to love him. That would take courage, too.

Duke or scholar, it mattered not. She loved him for the man he was. Unlike the beau ideal of the *ton*, he treated her on an equal footing. He listened to her. He joined in her whimsical play, and he shared her passion. There was so much she loved about him that, she realized with a start, it didn't matter that he was a duke. Her love saw through the outer trappings of rank and the shy manners of a student to the man behind those barriers.

Lydia sat up in the bed and hugged her knees to her breast. The cool night air brushed her heated skin and helped to clear her mind. Without realizing it, she had tried to reach that man. It was only when they were in their clearing in the woods that their souls had united. They were never at ease with each other elsewhere. Society's expectations had come between them and made him uneasy and her flirtatious. Well, society had now closed its doors to her. It no longer had a claim upon her actions. His refusal to redeem her had set that path.

Yet, Lydia acknowledged to the night, *I wish I could have married him.*

Brave resolutions were all well and good when made in the dark of the night, but the daylight weakened their strength and made it harder for one to walk down the town streets. Lydia and her mother were headed for the milliner's when Elizabeth Chandler stepped out of the shop's door.

"Elizabeth." Lydia greeted her. "How lovely to see you."

A startled look crossed the other girl's face, and she hesitated on the stoop. Then she turned back to speak with someone in the shop. "Come along now, Nancy. There's no need to wait for those purchases to be wrapped. They can be delivered to the house later."

"But, miss, don't you want them for tonight's musicale?" asked the voice of the unseen maid.

"No!" Elizabeth cast a superior look at Lydia. "We are leaving now."

"Yes, miss," came the subdued reply.

Elizabeth pulled her skirt close to her body and stepped past Lydia, her maid right behind her.

Her face burning, Lydia blocked Elizabeth's path. "Good afternoon, Elizabeth. How are you?"

The other girl turned her head away but said nothing.

"It is very rude not to respond to a greeting." Lydia's throat suddenly seemed clogged with tears. "I am looking forward to the musicale you are having tonight. Do you want me to sing?"

Elizabeth faced her then, dislike written plain upon her face. "If you show your face at our door, it will be shut in your face. You are no longer welcome at my musicale—or in my presence."

Lydia's mother gasped at such blunt speech.

After a moment to absorb the blow, Lydia moved aside. Elizabeth sailed by with her chin raised and her maid in tow. Together, Lydia and her mother watched them strut conspicuously down the street.

With her eyes glistening, her mother said, "Shall we discover what treasures await us inside?"

Lydia shook her head. "I think not. I have suddenly lost all appetite for fripperies. Can we return home instead?"

"Home? What do you want to do there?"

"Perhaps rest. I think I am developing a headache."

Her mother glanced down the street in Elizabeth's direction.

"Yes," Lydia said. "I think my head will hurt so badly I will not be able to attend tonight's musicale."

Her mother swallowed visibly. "I shall stay home to care for you. The Chandler musicale will be diminished by your absence. You have such a beautiful voice."

"If I feel better, I shall sing for you and Papa," Lydia said with as much lightness as she could.

"Thank you."

With their heads held high, the ladies started toward their carriage. Lydia looked back one more time, but Elizabeth was out of sight.

Lydia knew she would not be going to the musicale, nor would she be attending any of the other upcoming local functions. They were closed to her. She regretted their loss for her mother's sake and for her own. She had liked parties.

When they reached where the carriage was parked, her mother was handed in first and Lydia climbed in after. The driver settled into his seat and started the horses for home. There was no need to go shopping but for the dull reason of necessities. Why did she need anything new? No one would notice. Lydia was invisible now.

Looking out the window as the crowded town buildings gave way to the open countryside, Lydia realized she was her own person.

A sense of freedom surged through her like freshwater from the well. For the first time in her life, she no longer had to obey the endless strictures dictating what she could and could not do as a young lady. If she wanted to walk barefoot in the street, who could tell her no? If she wanted go sketching in the woods every day, why would anyone stop her? She could be ruined only once. Whatever she did from now on was her choice.

The only question remaining was, would Someone miss her at the musicale?

*   *   *

Where was Lydia? Winterbourne wondered. Sitting on the hard chair and listening to two girls exaggerate a ballad as if it were being sung in an opera, he kept an interest look pasted on his face. When he had accepted the invitation, he had understood Lydia was to be one of the singers. He had heard her voice was sweet and lyrical, much more appropriate to this ballad than the voices of the current singers.

Although the performance had already started, there was no sign of her, and that made him uneasy. He could not forget the memory of Josiah's pleading face as he begged for his daughter's marriage. Winterbourne refused to be coerced into a wedding, but he did not wish for Lydia to suffer. Despite her attempts to become his duchess, he cared for her. She was unlike any other woman he had met, a mixture of whimsy and manipulation.

Polite applause broke his reverie, and he joined in with relief. The two girls bowed and bowed at their reception until the bustle of people standing and starting conversations told them the recital was finished.

Winterbourne stood and looked for his host's family. He spotted the daughter of the house by the piano, although he would have preferred to speak with her mother. Mrs. Chandler would be the one who had prepared the guest list. She was talking with three other matrons. Since he was a duke, his approach would interrupt her conversation. She would not regard it as an imposition, but Winterbourne did not want his inquiry about Lydia overheard by avid ears.

Elizabeth arranged the music on the piano into a neat pile. She stopped immediately as he drew near and greeted him with a wide smile that displayed her teeth and reminded him of a predator.

"Your grace," she welcomed him, clearly pleased by his notice. "Did you enjoy the singing?"

"They did quite well," he lied.

"Yes, they are wonderful singers. It is a pretty concert when two sisters can mingle their voices in such a lovely fashion."

Would she have agreed with him if he had disparaged their performance? From the arch look she gave him, he thought she would echo whatever his opinion was. She made him feel uncomfortable, and he wished for Lydia.

Giving one last glance around the company gathered in the drawing room, he said, "I had understood Miss Grenville would be singing tonight, yet I do not see her."

Elizabeth stiffened and said in a low voice, "She is not here, your grace."

Without knowing why she did so, Winterbourne also lowered his voice. "Why not? Is she ill?"

"I prefer not to speak her name."

He drew back in surprise. "Are you not friends? What has happened?"

Elizabeth shifted on her feet, and from the pink staining her cheeks he knew her unease was not a pretense of agitation. "Please, your grace," she said. "It is not something I should talk about."

Her evasion awoke a strong sense of disquiet within him. Something was seriously wrong here. "Tell me about it."

She clutched her hands together and glanced toward her mother as if seeking succor. The woman still chatted with her friends, but Winterbourne spotted the gesture she made in her daughter's direction. She was obviously proud and pleased that the duke spoke to Elizabeth, and she wanted the other ladies to notice. However, she did not see the desperate look her daughter tossed her.

Winterbourne determined to untangle this evasion. Lydia's whereabouts should not be a mystery.

He offered Elizabeth his arm. "Miss Chandler, would you honor me by taking a turn around the room?"

She did not want to. He could tell from the quick looks that she kept giving her mother, but one of the advantages of being a duke was that Elizabeth could not refuse him, even if she did not like the direction of his conversation.

"Thank you, your grace."

She placed her hand on his arm, and they began to stroll. Several of the guests discreetly watched them while bending their heads close together. His lips tightened. He would never be at ease with being the center of everyone's attention.

"Tell me why Miss Grenville is not here," he demanded. Although his voice remained quiet, the steel in his tone was unmistakable.

"Your grace, she is not a comfortable topic for me. Can we not discuss something else? Music, perhaps?"

"No."

She sighed and looked at the floor. "She was not invited."

"Not invited? I thought she was numbered among your guests." He would never have come if he had known she was not going to be here. "Fanny said your mother had included her."

Elizabeth continued to watch her steps. "She was, but she was disinvited."

"Disinvited?" Shock halted his steps. "Why was her invitation rescinded?"

"Your grace, please don't ask me so many questions." Her wail was sincere, if muted. Like him, she was aware of the watching eyes and listening ears.

Plainly there was more to this tale. Winterbourne took Elizabeth's arm and firmly escorted her to a little alcove nestled next to the fireplace. A small couch sat there. He set her on it and then joined her. Because of the fire burning in the nearby hearth, the alcove was exceedingly warm, but it had the advantage of being available and under the eyes of numerous chaperones. They could see but could not hear what was said.

"Tell me," he commanded.

"Lydia Grenville is not a proper topic for a young lady."

Elizabeth made one last appeal with her eyes. Her big brown eyes with their dark lashes had no effect upon him. He wanted to see the one with golden curls, blue eyes, and fair complexion.

"I want the entire tale," he said.

When he remained implacable, her shoulders fell. "I had to disinvite her. I had no choice."

"If you invited her in the first place, certainly you had a choice about withdrawing the invitation."

She shook her head. Her curls did not dance the way Lydia's did. "No, your grace, I didn't. My mother took it back as soon as she heard the gossip. I can't be seen with Lydia anymore."

His brows drew together. "What gossip caused Lydia to be shunned?"

She pleated her skirt between her fingers.

"If you do not tell me, I will stand up right here and demand that all of your guests tell me. I am certain they have heard the same disgraceful stories as you. Do you want such a scene at your musicale?"

Her gaze flew to him in horror. "You wouldn't!"

He made as if to rise.

"No, don't!"

He paused partway up, and she surrendered.

"I mustn't be seen in Lydia's presence any longer," she said. "No respectable lady can, because Lydia has been secretly meeting a man in the woods."

"And for that reason you shrink from her presence?" A sick feeling rocked him. "What about the man? Do you avoid him, too?"

Elizabeth looked everywhere but at him.

"Was the man disinvited?" he demanded. "Was he?"

"You know he was not," she whispered.

Yes, he knew the invitation held for the man, and he knew why. Because he was the Duke of Winterbourne. Lydia was punished, while he escaped. Josiah had been right. Winterbourne had behaved badly.

Abruptly, he stood and bowed. "Thank you for inviting me this evening, but I find I must leave. I do not suit this company."

Her eyes widened. "Please, your grace, I meant no disrespect."

"No, not to me. But what is done to Lydia is also done to me." With that he turned and left the room.

On the ride home, revulsion for his actions mingled with his disgust for a society that would penalize the woman when the man was equally guilty. Yet he refused to push the blame solely on society. He had been wrong, and now he had to make it up to her.

He must marry her. He had thought he had a choice in the matter, but the scandal had forced his selection. He cared for Lydia too much to allow her ostracism to occur. Tomorrow he would call upon Grenville Manor, apologize for his error, and ask for Lydia's hand. It would be granted, because of the scandal and because he was a duke. With rueful acceptance, he resigned himself to his future.

In the morning, before he could implement his plans, Cecil stopped Winterbourne on the drive just as he was preparing to mount his horse and ride to the manor.

"Your grace, did you forget we planned to inspect Mr. Sutton's roof this morning?"

Winterbourne had forgotten. With one hand on the saddle and the other holding the reins, he was in no mood to accommodate Cecil's schedule. "He can wait. I have other plans."

"Indeed, your grace. When shall I tell him is more favorable?"

"I don't know. Sometime later."

"I will tell him," Cecil said smoothly. "Your grace will appear when you are ready. Mr. Sutton can certainly wait upon your convenience. The afternoon or the next day or even later, it should make no difference to him."

He looked at Cecil. His face remained bland, but Winterbourne was not fooled. His cousin meant for him to follow the timetable he had arranged. Winterbourne sighed. He could not be so inconsiderate of a farmer who likely had a wife who had spent yesterday baking in honor of the duke's impending visit.

"Very well, then. Get your horse. We shall inspect Mr. Sutton's roof this morning." He would go to Grenville Manor this afternoon, which was the more appropriate time for a call anyway.

At the Sutton farm, Winterbourne climbed the ladder and surveyed the roof. He could not tell if it was in good shape or not. Once he'd climbed down, Cecil went up. Then he and the farmer engaged in a detailed discussion of the roof's state, while Winterbourne sampled the biscuits with jam that Mrs. Sutton set before him. His conversation consisted solely of compliments on her cooking, which gratified her.

The ride back took them through the woods surrounding the castle. As their horses clomped through the trees, a pang shot through Winterbourne. Most of the leaves had fallen from the branches, leaving them bare. No secrets could hide in the forest now. The game in the fairy princess's enchanted domain was over. Reality had intruded. Soon they would reach the outlying gardens of the castle, and he would leave for his call on Lydia.

Cecil reined his horse. "Excuse me, your grace. I think my horse has picked up a stone."

Winterbourne halted his horse and groaned inwardly. Another delay. "You had better make certain."

His cousin dismounted and picked up the left foreleg. He brushed away some dirt. "I can't tell if it's bruised or not. Maybe you should take a look."

Winterbourne wanted to get home. He wanted to ask Lydia to marry him. He wanted to start the life he had planned, but he could not rudely leave Cecil behind. He dismounted. "Let me see."

Cecil stepped behind as Winterbourne lifted the leg. He ran his finger around the hoof but saw nothing to cause the horse distress. "It appears to be fine," he said.

He released the leg and started to straighten. A sudden pain exploded in his head. Black spots with jagged red lines filled his vision until the dots swam together. He slumped to the ground as the darkness overwhelmed his senses.

Chapter Fourteen

*H*is head hurt. That was the first thing Winterbourne was aware of when his eyes blinked open. The sudden flash of pain, which had tumbled him into unconsciousness, had subsided into a throbbing in his skull like that of a team of horses galloping over a road. He shook his head, winced, and closed his eyes until the spike of pain hammered into his head had lessened. His eyes opened more carefully the second time.

Glancing around at the rakes, hoes, and shovels lining the walls, he deduced he was in a garden shed. The smell of wet dirt permeated the air. Mud streaked his breeches, and bits of dirt and leaves clung to his clothes. Obviously he had been dragged here. But by whom? And for what purpose?

Winterbourne struggled to rise and failed. His hands were bound behind his back. He tugged them in disbelief. The rope held fast. Some plot was afoot, and its result was not meant for his benefit. Fear curled within him like a ribbon of smoke. His mouth dried, and he licked his lips. What was going to happen to him? He did not want to wait and find out. He yanked frantically to free his hands. The need to escape overpowered any sensible thought. Pushing and pulling, his body twisted into contortions only an acrobat could execute.

His struggles sent a hoe crashing from the wall. Its wooden handle narrowly missed hitting his head. Gasping from his exertions, he looked at it and steadied. He must think logically. He must calm down. Losing his head in the situation would not help. He filled his lungs and gradually exhaled.

Think. He must think. If he could determine why someone would do this to him, then he should know who the perpetrator was.

Winterbourne considered. He could no longer deny that the shot in the woods had been aimed at him. Thank God Lydia had not been hurt. What was the villain after? Money? Could he have been kidnapped for ransom? He certainly was a wealthy man, with all of the dukedom's assets at his disposal. But who could have known where would be today? Had someone been trailing him? Following him without his knowing it?

That was possible. Certainly he was not looking to spot someone following him. He had made a mistake in so lightly disregarding that shot. Yet, if this person had kidnapped him, where was Cecil? Winterbourne was the only one in this shed. Had Cecil been hurt or killed?

He tamped down the concern. Likely Cecil was fine. Anyone seeking knowledge of the dukedom's affairs would soon learn that his cousin managed the finances. If money was expected for the duke's return, Cecil was the one who would arrange payment.

Except why would someone attack him in Cecil's presence?

The only logical answer was that the someone was Cecil.

At the sureness coursing through his bones, Winterbourne knew his conclusion was correct. And once he knew who had done it, the why of it was plain. Cecil wanted to be duke. He wanted to make the decisions. He wanted to build that blasted canal. It was not kidnapping for a ransom that was planned, and that made his situation even more dangerous. A demand for ransom implied his life had value.

Well, Winterbourne would not submit without a fight. He must escape. He looked around the shed and realized his cousin must have been rattled when he dragged his body in here. The shed was filled with gardening implements, tools designed to cut the earth. They would cut his bonds.

The hoe that had nearly hit him lay beside him. It took some twisting of his body, but at last he had it braced against the wall and his hands positioned against the blade. Cecil always took care of the estate's details, and his concern trickled down to the gardener's care of his tools. The sharp edge of the hoe sliced the rope's strands. In a short time Winterbourne was free.

Tossing the remnants from his wrists, he scrambled to his feet and went to the door. Cracking it open, he saw no one else was around. The shed was one that stood at the far end of the estate lawns. He and Cecil must have been near it when the blow came.

Winterbourne debated. Should he leave or wait here to see what Cecil's plans involved? Leaving the shed would certainly disrupt them and surprise his cousin. It would be better to surprise Cecil here. Winterbourne liked the prospect of having the upper hand. He would wait for Cecil's return. His head throbbed and his wrists ached. If the wait grew too long, then he would leave.

The sun had begun to set when he spotted Cecil riding across the lawn. Winterbourne leaned the hoe against the wall and resumed his position on the floor with his hands thrust behind him.

His cousin entered and stopped short.

"Cecil!" Winterbourne exclaimed.

"You are awake, I see." Cecil reached into his coat, pulled out a pistol, and pointed it shakily.

"So you are the villain who did this to me." Winterbourne shifted on the ground. "Why did you hit me and tie me up thus?"

"You wouldn't understand. You never listened to me."

"I have no choice but to listen to you now."

"You don't, do you?" With a satisfied smirk, Cecil walked over and stood above him. Winterbourne considered kicking his cousin's legs out from under him, but the pistol he held gave him pause.

"You had everything," Cecil burst out. "And you didn't care about it."

"Is this about that canal? Because I don't understand how treating me like this will get it built."

"It's not just the canal. It's your whole approach to the dukedom. You don't care about it."

"But I do!" Winterbourne sat up as much as his position would allow. Cecil could not make such statements without him protesting. "You have been teaching me about its management."

"Yes, we discuss projects, and then you veto them."

"I agreed to investigating the mill possibility."

"You say no to everything." Cecil glowered at him. "I wish you *had* gone to Greece. Everything would have been perfect then."

"Sorry to disappoint you," Winterbourne said. He would not reveal how Lydia's influence had driven him to find an escape. If only he could be certain of her feelings for him! Resolutely he set thoughts of her aside. Right now he had to concentrate on Cecil's intentions. "The dukedom does belong to me."

Cecil stiffened. "I should be the duke. I have all the qual-
ifications."

"The only obstacle being that I am the present duke,"
Winterbourne observed. "After all, you are my heir."

"Yes."

Winterbourne met Cecil's gaze steadily. "So do you plan
to kill me? Commit murder here?" He gathered himself to attack. The pistol now dangled from his cousin's hand. If Cecil
intended to fire, he would fight.

Cecil's eyes slid away. "I suppose I must. I don't like the
idea of killing you."

"Good of you," Winterbourne muttered.

The other man ignored him. "I don't really want the title.
You could have kept that if you'd left me in charge. Your trip
to Greece was the perfect solution. And then you didn't go."
Turning his back, he walked toward the door. "I don't want
to kill you, but I must. It's the only way that I can see to the
good of the estate. I must tighten my courage. Gird my loins
for the distasteful task. I must do what has to be done."

During Cecil's musings, Winterbourne gathered his legs
beneath him and stood. He grabbed the hoe. As Cecil turned,
Winterbourne used all his strength to swing the hoe's handle
against the arm holding the pistol.

"Ow!" Cecil cried, dropping his gun. He looked at him in
amazement. "You were free the whole time."

Winterbourne held the hoe at the ready in case he needed
a weapon. "I will not wait passively for the fate you intend."

"I wanted to take care of the estate. That's all."

"It's *my* property, Cecil," he said quietly. "I am Winterbourne."

His cousin's face seemed to crumple like a wad of paper.
"It's not fair. There's so much I could have done."

Hearing the defeat in the other man's voice, Winterbourne

relaxed his tight grip on the handle. "I'm sorry," he said and was amazed to find that the statement was true. He felt only pity for Cecil. He picked up the gun and added, "Sometimes life is not fair."

"What do you intend to do with me?" Cecil's shoulders sagged. "You need to turn me in."

Winterbourne looked at the gun he held and found he did not know what he should do to his cousin. Yes, Cecil had tried to kill him—twice—but he had not succeeded. And Winterbourne could understand the railing at fate. He had done it himself when he inherited the dukedom. It was Cecil who had forced him to take up his responsibilities. The canal was the outward sign of the rift between them. A wise manager used his resources, and Cecil's knowledge was too valuable to waste. Surely the dukedom owned an estate in some remote section of Scotland where Cecil could expend his energies for profit.

Winterbourne eyed his cousin. "I know just how to use you."

Despite his intentions, two days later Winterbourne still had not been able to ride to Grenville Manor and request Lydia's hand in marriage. It was Cecil's fault. Ever since the attack, Winterbourne had been buried under the management of the dukedom. He wanted Lydia, but he had to admit he missed Cecil's abilities.

His cousin was on his way to the estate in Scotland, where he would have free rein in supervising the property. Winterbourne figured it would become a modern model of farm management. Cecil could do great work.

Looking at the piles of paper cluttering his formerly polished desktop, Winterbourne knew he would have to hire a new secretary—and quickly. He did not possess the skill to deal with these details of his properties. Decisions had to be made, but he was lost in the morass piled before him. And he knew that in the anteroom at least three people waited to present their petitions.

It wasn't only the questions of how to handle his properties that weighed on his mind. Cecil bothered him. He had seemed content with his duties, delving through the old records, handling the correspondence from the tenants and others who worked in the dukedom, and preparing his interminable reports. Cecil's life had suited him.

What, Winterbourne wondered, had he done to make Cecil hate him so deeply that he attempted murder?

To be honest, his plot was likely the only thing Cecil ever planned that did not have his usual success. He had admitted to firing the shot in the woods, but when the moment came and his prey lay tied up at his feet, Cecil had not been able to pull the trigger. As much as he wanted his vision for the dukedom to prevail, he could not grab it.

He turned Cecil's words in his mind over and over. *You had everything*.

Did he mean the dukedom's wealth? Winterbourne shook his head. It was not the money Cecil wanted, but the power. Winterbourne held that power and he had used it, but wealth and power had not brought satisfaction to his spirit. He was the Duke of Winterbourne, and it was not enough. Maybe if Cecil had succeeded, he would have learned the same truth, but Winterbourne doubted it. Minutiae satisfied Cecil.

He picked up the letter resting on top of a pile and began to read. It was his duty to address the concerns of those who depended upon him. Yet his mind kept wandering. After twice rereading the paper written in wavering handwriting, Winterbourne threw it down in disgust.

This was not how a duke should conduct his affairs. This

concern over details was Cecil's method of handling the dukedom, and Winterbourne was done with Cecil. He must hire that secretary. He would draft an advertisement for one immediately.

Pleased with his decision, Winterbourne searched the top of his desk for a clean sheet of paper on which to write. He shoved the piles aside and paged through them. The stack of constant invitations he ignored. He was not going anywhere if Lydia was not included.

Then he spotted a sheet written in his own hand back when he had listed the pros and cons of Lydia as a wife. He leaned back in his chair and considered what he had written. Her physical attributes were there, of course, but he remembered that even as he wrote them, he had known they did not capture Lydia's heart.

The positive side was longer than the negative. In fact, that side was blank, but he knew what he had dared not write. He had feared Lydia saw only the rank of duchess, not the man who went with it. He had feared to trust her.

With the suddenness of a blazing lightning strike, he realized he had focused on his rank as much as any matchmaking mama. Every time he was with Lydia, he examined her every gesture through the lens of her social expectations. And that lens had become his prison. Well, he had recognized its limitations and he was free now. Free to—to what?

He smoothed the paper in his hand and remembered Lydia. When he had first met her, she did not know his true identity. Once it had been revealed, she had attempted to gain his attention through her coquetry.

It had not worked because he had always recognized its falseness, but there were other times when her social mask dropped. She was always true as Lydia-of-the-woods. Sometimes that nymph appeared even in social settings. Could he forget the dance they had sat out together? He had revealed his frustration with the illogicality of emotion. With whom else could he share such a concept? She saw past the rank, but he had not. Such a woman was the mate of his heart. He loved her. All this time, love for her had flourished within him, and he had confused it with passion.

Passion did exist. Those two kisses proved it. He had so concentrated on it that he had overlooked why it existed. Those emotions did not ignite in him for any other woman. Only Lydia. And only because he loved her.

He must call upon Grenville Manor immediately. Forget these dusty duties. He needed to gain his lover as his bride. A quick glance at the clock confirmed it was not too late for an afternoon call.

He bounded from the library and raced to his rooms to dress. He stopped long enough to poke his head into the anteroom, where he announced to those waiting to see him, "I regret I cannot see you today. Please return once I have hired a secretary."

Then he was gone, ready to put himself into his valet's hands. If he hurried, he could make that call at Grenville Manor.

After all, a suitor must look his best.

Chapter Fifteen

*O*nce the butler recognized Winterbourne when he called at Grenville Manor, he immediately showed him to the drawing room. The last time he had been here, Winterbourne had faced the unmasking of his deception. He had been so tense he had paid no attention to his surroundings and focused instead upon Lydia and her reaction.

Once again he would be facing her, and once again he was not sure what her reaction would be. He had dressed in his finest clothes, although whether it was to impress her or reassure himself, he did not bother to analyze.

Unable to sit and wait, he paced around the room. A china figurine on a table caught his notice. It showed an overdressed shepherdess with a blissful look on her face. A fanciful portrayal. One that would be at home in the fairy princess's domain. He had never seen any shepherdess garbed so richly—or appearing so contented—but Lydia had taught him to see beyond the concrete. There existed a whole world he had never studied at university. The world of feeling, of emotion.

Lydia had introduced him to passion, and with her he had found love. At last, he knew his own mind—and his heart.

With her by his side, they would explore this other world for the rest of their lives. He was here to ask—no, beg—for Lydia's hand.

The door crashed open. Winterbourne turned to see Josiah Grenville stomp into the room. There was no sign of Lydia.

"What are you doing here?" Josiah demanded. His bushy eyebrows slammed together to form a single fierce line.

Winterbourne stiffened but knew he deserved her father's rude treatment. Bowing, he said, "Good afternoon, sir."

"I asked you a question."

"You have every right to be angry—"

"You are not welcome here."

Josiah grabbed him by the arm and pulled him toward the door. Shock stunned Winterbourne, and he allowed himself to be led. Then his senses recovered. Winterbourne yanked his arm free.

"I beg your pardon," he said. "I know you are angry with me, and you have every right to be. My behavior has been abominable. I offer my deepest apologies."

"I don't want your regrets. I want you out of my house." Josiah reached for him again.

Winterbourne lifted his walking stick to fend off his grasp. "I came to call on Miss Grenville."

"You're not going anywhere near my daughter." Josiah made another grab, but Winterbourne evaded his reach. "I want you out of my house. Do I need to summon the servants to have you thrown out?"

"That is not necessary," Winterbourne said. Desperation shot into his voice. He had not foreseen that he might not be able to see her. "I wish to speak with Lydia for only a moment."

Josiah looked at him and shouted, "Newton, come here."

The butler appeared in the doorway. "Yes, sir."

"His grace needs assistance in leaving the house." Josiah grabbed Winterbourne's arm again and directed the butler. "You take the other one."

The butler hesitated.

"Mr. Grenville, sir," Winterbourne said, "if you will only let me speak with Lydia."

"No. Take his other arm," Josiah ordered the butler.

Winterbourne tried to pull away, but their grips were too strong. He considered hitting them with his walking stick, but he was on a quest for the man's daughter in marriage. Blows did not seem the appropriate etiquette.

"If you will not let me speak with her, then listen to me," he shouted. "I want to marry your daughter."

Josiah hesitated but did not loosen his grasp. "Marry Lydia? Why? Why now, after you have ruined her?"

Winterbourne planted his feet. "She is not ruined. She is the most beautiful woman in the world."

"Fine words," Josiah sneered. "You have already hurt her past counting. You will not hurt my puss even further. You are done playing with her feelings."

With a mighty shove, he sent Winterbourne stumbling through the drawing room door. Recovering, he looked up and saw Lydia with her mother standing on the steps halfway down.

"Lydia!" he cried and started toward her.

Her father was too quick for him and interposed his bulk between them. "You are to have nothing more to do with my daughter."

"I heard the commotion," she said. "What is happening?"

Winterbourne looked past him. "Lydia, I must speak with you."

She eyed him uncertainly. "What could you possibly say to me?"

"I only need to speak with you. That's all," he cried. "Just give me a moment."

"Don't let him bother you," Josiah said. "He will be gone from here directly. I'll protect you from the likes of him."

He nodded to the butler, and the two men seized him again. Winterbourne tried to pull free and dropped his walking stick in the effort.

He had to speak with Lydia. He had to let her know of his love, but it couldn't be said here. As he struggled against her father and the butler, he called out, "Meet me."

"She's not meeting you again," Josiah declared with a firm grip on the duke's arm.

Winterbourne ignored him. It was Lydia who mattered. "I will wait for you."

"You will wait in vain," Josiah said and shoved. Winterbourne was pushed out the front door and sent sprawling down the steps. His walking stick was tossed out after him.

"Don't come calling again," Josiah warned him.

The door slammed shut.

Winterbourne picked himself up from the drive and brushed the bits of gravel and dirt from his clothes. His hand stung where it had hit the sharp stones. One sleeve of his jacket had ripped at the shoulder, but he did not care. His valet could repair it. How could he repair his attempted proposal?

He loved Lydia. He wanted to marry her, to share their lives together, to explore the worlds of passion and of thought. Yet he would never have the opportunity to tell her. Her father would not bestow her hand upon him, despite Winterbourne's shouted offer of marriage. Since Lydia was banned from local society, he would not meet her at the parties. The one place where he could meet her was in the woods where it had all begun.

He tightened his jaw. The woods. That was the proper place to offer her his heart and beg for her hand in return. He tugged his horse's reins free from the railing where he had tied them. He knew what to do. He had told Lydia where he would be. She could not reach the clearing today. Her father would prevent her. But there was tomorrow. Maybe she could slip away then. He would wait for her. Tomorrow or the next day or beyond, he would be there.

The only question was, would she come?

He arrived early in the morning, long before he could expect Lydia to come. Yet, in eagerness and fear, he did not want to miss her. He had brought her blanket and laid it upon the ground. He leaned against a tree so he could watch the direction she would take.

She did not come. The sun climbed higher in a sky heavy with clouds portending snow. He sat there for so long and was so motionless that a squirrel climbed down a tree. The animal paused on the ground and eyed Winterbourne suspiciously. When he did not move and only barely breathed, the squirrel nosed around the roots of the tree for nuts. After a minute of searching, the squirrel apparently decided not to risk any further proximity to the man and dashed away, chattering his displeasure.

The interlude with the squirrel was the only bit of entertainment Winterbourne enjoyed. It was quiet and cold in the clearing, but he was warmly dressed. The skin on his face gradually became chilled, so he wrapped the muffler around his neck higher. He was not going to leave. His love for her was true and constant. If—when—Lydia came, he would be here. If it did not happen today, then tomorrow.

*   *   *

At first Lydia did not see him as she walked through the woods. Yesterday's scene when her father had thrown the duke out of the manor had shocked her. Winterbourne's desperate plea to speak with her had intrigued her. What did he want to say?

When she asked her father, he squeezed her tight and said, "Don't worry your pretty head about *him*, puss. I took care of him. He isn't going to hurt you any longer."

Her curiosity increased. If Winterbourne had something he wanted to tell her, she thought she wanted to hear it. There was only one place where they could meet—at the clearing in the woods.

Did she want to go there? Lydia picked up her winter coat. Who could stop her? She had no reputation left to ruin and thus was free to do as she wished.

She left the manor without difficulty, although she had been prepared to argue if one of her parents had appeared. No one did, and Lydia picked her solitary way over the familiar route.

At first, she thought she'd been mistaken in her reasoning, for she did not see him sitting on the ground. Then a large brown bulk moved and she recognized him.

She could not prevent the delight gushing through her, but she did not rush to him. With deliberate steps, she entered the clearing at the edge and stood apart.

He rose as soon as he saw her. "Lydia, you came."

"I thought you asked me to."

"I feared you didn't want to see me again." He started to go to her, but halted when she held up her hand.

"I wanted to speak to you," he said.

"You can say your piece from there." When he moved, she said, "Don't come any closer."

"Why not?" he asked in a soft voice. If the woods had not been so quiet, she would have had to lean forward to hear him.

"I don't want you near. I can't think when you are close enough to kiss."

"I want to kiss you," he said in the same low voice. "In fact, I want to marry you."

She stiffened with wariness. Seeing it, he bent a knee before her. "Lydia, please. I am asking you to be my wife."

The words thrilled her like a great rush of wind whipping through her. She wanted to believe them because she loved him. "Why? Why do you want to marry me?"

Surprise crossed his face and he said, "Did I not tell you? I love you."

Oh, how she had longed to hear him say that! Her resistance was weakening. With an inner struggle, she managed to say, "You refused me when my father begged you to wed me."

"I was wrong. I tried to apologize for my behavior yesterday, but he would not listen or let me tell you. I want to marry you and cherish you for the rest of my life."

She took a step toward him. "I thought you feared my designs upon your rank."

For a moment he gazed at her. Then he took off his hat and set it on the ground. Standing, he began to unwind the scarf from around his neck.

Bewildered, she asked, "What are you doing?"

He dropped the scarf on the ground, and unbuttoning his coat, he shrugged out of it with difficulty. When that lay on the ground, his waistcoat joined it until he stood before her clad in his shirt and breeches. The cold air coiled around him and he shivered.

"Lydia," he said, "when we first met, this was how I was dressed."

"It was warmer then. You're going to catch a sickness dressed like that." She went to pick up his coat. His hands on her shoulders stopped her.

"No," he said. "Back then, you knew nothing more about me than what you saw and we discussed. There was no rank between us. Just a man and a woman. That is how I come to you today."

Breathless, she waited as he took up her hands in his.

Gazing into her eyes, he said, "Lydia, this man asks this woman to be his wife because he loves her."

She looked at him with wonder. His hair was tousled, but his eyes were clear and steady. Dressed as when they first met, he now appeared like Alexander. He had shed the trappings of the Duke of Winterbourne, yet Lydia realized that neither Alexander nor the duke stood before her. Only a man named John who proposed to a woman named Lydia. Nothing else mattered.

"Yes," she said with a sigh. "I love you, and I will marry you." Winter might have been coming on, but inside her, joy bloomed as if spring had burst free.

"I will love you for all the rest of my days." A rueful smile crossed his lips. "With all of my education, I was actually illiterate when it came to reading the love right in front of me. I am not worthy of you."

She put her fingers to his lips. "Hush. There is no rank or questions of betterment between us. It is only you and I—and our love."

He bent his head toward her, and she met him halfway. Her arms pulled him close, even as he pressed her to him. There was no more need for words. Love had matched them equally as partners for life.

The first big snowflakes drifted down, sprinkling the trees with the promise of fairy magic. More of the flakes fell, faster and faster, until they formed a curtain shielding the man and the woman in their own world.

"This debut novel heralds the arrival of a major new Regency writer."
—*Dallas Morning News*

THE SPINSTER AND THE WASTREL

by
Louise Bergin

When Nigel Montfort dies, leaving his estate to Miss Courtney, she establishes a school. Left out of the will, the prodigal nephew Gerald is outraged—until Courtney gives him a lesson in love.

"Lively Regency...
A new voice to watch."
—Amanda McCabe

0-451-21012-3

Available wherever books are sold or at
www.penguin.com